Cherokee Blake

Annette McLean was in deep trouble for her father had been murdered, and their cattle stolen. Worse still, she had been brutally assaulted by a gang of men. Now she alone can take revenge for virtually no one believes her and even the local sheriff is refusing to do anything because one of the men Annette has named as an attacker is Buddy Devenish, the son of the most powerful man in the county.

But help is to hand when US Marshal Clay Blake arrives in town, and believes Annette's story. Clay Blake is one-quarter Cherokee Indian and an all-over tough guy who will stop at nothing to see justice done.

Now, perhaps, Annette will get her day in court, and see Buddy and his vicious cohorts rot in jail – or die of lead poisoning.

Cherokee Blake

A.C. DUNN

A Black Horse Western

ROBERT HALE · LONDON

Typeset by
Derek Doyle & Associates, Liverpool.
Printed and bound in Great Britain by
Antony Rowe Limited, Wiltshire

One

The stage was late. It was nearly six o'clock when the few passengers alighted outside Soames' Hotel in El Paso, Texas. The weather was pleasant, it was nearly spring, but a long coach trip was a drain on anyone.

The man stood in the street and removed his duster. He was of average height but strongly built. What drew the attention was his face, dark-skinned, with brown piercing eyes. His hair was jet-black and reached below his shoulders. He wore a three-piece black suit with a frock-coat. A well-cared for .45 was on his left side. When he bent to pick up his bags his coat fell open, revealing a shoulder holster under his right arm. He carried a rifle in a full-length, fringed, buckskin scabbard. On top of his carpet-bag lay a short-barrelled shotgun.

He entered the hotel and placed his bag on the floor and his rifle on the bar. He asked the barman for a room. He signed the register, C. Blake.

'Can I get a bath?' he asked the barman.

'Sure, out back, water should be hot by now. You want to order supper? It'll be ready in an hour.'

C. Blake ordered a big steak with everything.

He reached down for his bag. From behind, someone grabbed his rifle off the bar.

'Lookee here, Jeff,' a voice said. 'Ain't this a nice outfit? How come an Indian owns somethin' like this?'

'Put it down,' C. Blake said in a soft voice.

'You speakin' to me, Indian? You wanna watch your place, boy.'

In the blink of an eye, C. Blake grabbed the Greener from the top of his carpet-bag and clubbed his protagonist to the ground. He cocked the shotgun and pointed it at the prostrate man's companions.

'Don't die for him, boys. I pull these triggers, you'll be spread all over like a bad coat of paint.'

The two young men stood with their hands well away from their guns.

'Pick my rifle up,' C. Blake said. One young man did so. 'Now pick your friend up.' They did so, and departed quickly.

'On your feet, stranger,' someone said.

C. Blake looked up from his meal to see a sheriff and two deputies, all carrying rifles.

'I'm eating, Sheriff, what do you want?'

'You're under arrest for assault.'

C. Blake smiled and continued to eat. 'You won't shoot me, Sheriff, I know it and you know it. Why don't you sit down while I finish this fine meal?'

'Pat him down, Roy,' the sheriff said to one of his deputies.

Roy put his rifle down and drew his revolver. He cocked it and stuck it against the seated man's head. He proceeded to search him. First, he removed the man's sidearm and a Bowie knife. He threw open C. Blake's coat. 'Look at this, Sheriff, a shoulder harness. Our Injun is a real desperado, I think.'

'Get on with it, Roy.'

Roy reached into the seated man's inside pocket and removed his wallet.

'Look at that, Sheriff,' Roy pronounced as he flipped open the wallet. 'Must be five hundred dollars.' He jabbed C. Blake in the neck with his revolver, 'You rob a bank, Injun?' Roy removed another smaller wallet. 'What have we here?' he asked no one in particular. He let the wallet fall open, revealing a round silver badge. 'Well, well,' Roy said, 'You kill a marshal Injun?' He handed the badge to the sheriff.

'This yours?' the sheriff asked C. Blake, who had continued to eat while he was being searched.

'Yes.'

'What's your name?'

'Clay Blake.'

The sheriff paled noticeably. 'Oh shit,' he said. 'You're Cherokee Blake, aren't you?'

'I'm called that, yes.'

The sheriff lowered the hammer on his rifle. 'Go have a drink,' he said to his deputies.

'But, Sheriff . . .' Roy protested.

'Go on, go on. He's a Federal Marshal, do as I say,' the sheriff replied angrily. 'All right, Marshal, what do you want?'

The marshal put his fingers to his lips. 'When I'm finished eating,' he said.

The sheriff sat and watched Clay Blake eat; he sure enjoyed his food. The sheriff dug out his makings and started to build a cigarette.

'Don't smoke, please, inhaling someone else's smoke makes me cough. Disgusting habit, smoking,' Clay said, without looking up.

At last he finished his meal and drank the remnants of a glass of beer. A waitress removed his plate.

'Any pie?' he asked. He ordered the apple with cream, and coffee with milk and sugar. 'How about you, Sheriff?' The sheriff ordered black coffee.

Another ten minutes and Clay Blake was finished eating. 'That's better,' he said. 'Right now, Sheriff Dave Miller, isn't it?'

'Yes, and I don't like being kept waiting, by anyone.'

'Fair enough, Sheriff,' the marshal replied with a cold smile. 'But you barged in on me, remember?'

'So what do you want?'

'Annette McLean, know her?'

'Yes.'

'She wrote to the governor, stating that she reported to you that her father had been murdered by five men, who then stole their herd of cattle. That was after they'd held her prisoner for four days, and treated her in the vilest way imaginable. Ring any bells?'

9

The sheriff laughed, 'Is that why you're here? Well you've had a long trip for nothing.'

'Did you look into it?'

'Yeah, I looked into it, I think she's gone mad. Seems her pa is dead, right enough, and I reckon it tipped her over the edge. She showed me a pile of stones, said it was his grave. Probably was. It smelled like hell.'

'You didn't exhume him?'

'No.'

'So that's it? You dismissed the whole thing as the ravings of a lunatic?'

'Yeah. Besides, I know those boys, might be a bit wild, but they'd never do anything like she said.'

'So you're telling me that she came into your office, and told you in front of your deputies, that she had been violently raped by a gang of men, and you think she made it up?'

The sheriff looked uncomfortable. 'Well, yeah.'

'Well, you're right about one thing, she'd have to be crazy to embarrass herself like that. Would it interest you to know that a herd of two thousand, two hundred and nine cattle, with a thistle brand, were sold in Abilene on the fifth of August last year? Thistle is the McLean's brand, isn't it?'

'Yeah, but that don't prove anything.'

'Not by itself, no. But I have a declaration signed by the buyer, in the presence of a judge, that he bought the cattle from five men. Two were about my size, called themselves Ted and Mike Smith. Another was big and balding, looked like a farmer. Another was called Bud, he wore a pearl-handled six shooter, butt forward on his left hip. He laughed a lot, apparently. The fifth man was of slight build, wore black, and twin guns. That sound like the men this poor demented woman described to you?'

The sheriff was even more uncomfortable. 'Well, yeah, she accused Ted and Mike Murphy, Jack Hunt, Bud Devenish and Billy Watts, he's the gunman, supposed to be Buddy's minder.'

'Why does this Buddy have a minder?'

'Colonel Devenish hired him to keep Buddy out of trouble. Personally, I think Buddy's a bit light on.'

Clay Blake just stared at the sheriff. 'This woman reported all this to you and you did nothing? That's amazing, it really is.'

'Look here, Blake,' the sheriff blustered, 'I don't take orders from you. I did what I thought was best.'

'You did nothing!' the marshal spat at him.

'Because it would have been her word against

11

theirs. Besides, I have to get re-elected, you don't. Colonel Devenish pulls a lot o' weight in this county.'

'Good thing Annette McLean can't vote, isn't it? This Devenish, what's he a colonel of?'

'Talk is that Sam Houston made him a colonel during the war with Mexico.'

Clay Blake stretched in his chair. 'In other words, this Devenish has you all bluffed, so son Bud can get away with anything. Is that right?'

'No, it's not.'

The marshal slammed his hand on the table. 'Yes it is! It doesn't matter if this Devenish is the president, he's still subject to the law and so is his son. Shit!'

'I'll go and talk to him, then, if that's what you want.'

'No you won't, you stay away from all of them, and don't tell your deputies. If any of these men disappear suddenly, I'll arrest you, is that clear?'

'All right, all right. Anyhow, the Murphy brothers are gone.'

'Don' t you worry about them, I know where to scoop them up when I want them.' Clay stood up. 'I'm for bed. Sharpen up, Sheriff, everyone is entitled to protection under the law.'

The marshal turned his back on the sheriff,

and moved to where the deputies were leaning against the bar. With blinding speed he hammered Roy on the jaw, knocking him to the floor.

'You ever hold a gun to my head again, I suggest you pull the trigger, or I'll make you eat it.'

Roy's drinking companions all gathered around. Clay Blake removed his small wallet from his pocket and let it fall open.

'My name is Clay Blake, people call me Cherokee, I'm a federal marshal. I don't like people who stick guns in my face, and I don't like Indian jokes.' He looked at the men standing between him and the staircase. 'Now, get out of my way.'

They did so.

Ｔᴡᴏ

Clay slept late. After a leisurely breakfast he strolled to the telegraph office and sent several messages. The operator looked at him enquiringly.

'Those messages are confidential. If they get out, I'll know where to come,' Clay told him.

'Yes, sir,' the operator replied.

Next, he asked directions to the doctor's residence. Doctor James O'Day was a rotund, happy-looking, middle-aged man.

'You don't look sick,' the doctor told Clay.

'No, Doc, I'm fine, thanks. I'm Clay Blake, I'm a federal marshal. I'd like to talk to you about Annette McLean.'

The doctor was instantly suspicious.

'What about her?'

Clay gave the doctor a brief smile. 'Don't get your hackles up, Doc, I haven't met the lady, but I assure you I'm on her side.'

'Why?' the doctor asked, still suspicious.

'You're making this hard, Doc. All right, I've read her letter, I've read your report of her injuries. I've been to Kansas and I know that her cattle were sold there, by the men she claims were her attackers. I've been on a stagecoach for three weeks to get here, because I believe her, and I didn't come all this way so you could dance me around, *comprende*?'

The doctor smiled, 'Fair enough, Marshal. What do you want to know?' He invited Clay to sit.

'I've spoken to the sheriff,' the marshal began. 'He says Miss McLean is crazy. Is he right, do you think?'

'No, he's not right, not at the moment anyway. But she could end up that way.'

'Why do you think that?'

'Because no one else believes her. Because she demeaned herself by reporting it all to the sheriff. Do you know what happened? That stupid Roy Wallace asked her for a demonstration of what the men did to her. Can you imagine how that made her feel? Now she just stays at home. My wife and I try to get out to see her every week and take her some food. But she's going downhill and there's nothing I can do for her. I'm very worried about her. It's terrible, just terrible.'

'Well, if it helps any, Doc, the governor was concerned enough to have a marshal assigned to the case and I believe her. If I do say so myself, I get results. It won't be the first time I've started with nothing, believe me.'

The doctor smiled. 'I'll bet that's right, Marshal.'

'So, we've established that she needs help and I'm it. What do you suggest I do?'

'Well, you'll have to win her trust, that'll be hard. Then you have to prove what she says is right, in a court of law. That'll be hard. Then you've got to stay alive long enough to do it. Sounds simple to me.'

Clay laughed. He lunched with the doctor and his wife. The doctor gave him a bottle of sleeping-potion to administer to Annette, if possible. He gave Clay directions to the ranch. Clay hired a buggy, bought supplies, then headed out.

It was near to five o'clock when he drove into the deserted yard of Thistle Ranch. He headed the horse towards the house. A bullet threw up dust just in front of his horse. The animal ignored it and plodded on. Clay reined in alongside the porch.

'Miss McLean. I'm Clay Blake, I'm a federal marshal,' he called out. No reply.

He pulled out his small wallet and threw it on to the porch near the door.

'There are my credentials, Annette. You wanted help and I'm it. Shoot me, and the next lawman you see will have a warrant for your arrest, then you'll never get justice. Think it over. I'll be in your barn having a lie-down. If I leave, I won't be back.'

Clay put up the horse and spread his bedroll on the ground.

It was nearly dusk when she came. Clay lay with his eyes shut for a minute while the young woman just stood there. When he opened his eyes, he wasn't ready for the sight of Annette McLean. She was about five feet eight inches tall and her clothes hung off her like rags on a scarecrow. Her hair was a mess, her face was gaunt and her sunken eyes were ringed by dark circles. She looked appalling, Clay thought.

'What sort of marshal are you? I could have killed you,' she whispered.

Clay brought his left hand up from his side; he was holding a six-gun.

'You've been standing there for about a minute. If you had blinked wrong, I'd have shot you. I want to help you, Annette, but that doesn't include dying for you.'

Just a glimmer of a smile crossed her face.

'Come to the house,' she said, then turned on her heel and walked away.

Clay carried the supplies he had brought into the house. The place was a mess, the stove cold. He started a fire and put water on to boil. Annette stood at the window.

'If you want something to eat, you'll have to make it. I have to keep watch.'

Clay stood in front of her.

'No, you don't, I'm here now. No one will try anything while I'm here with you.'

For the first time she looked at him with her sad eyes.

'Yes, they will.'

'No, they won't,' Clay said sharply. 'Give me your rifle.'

She didn't move. Clay prised her fingers from around the weapon. One big tear rolled down her cheek. Clay put the rifle on the table and turned to Annette, taking her in his arms.

'Let me go,' she whispered.

'I won't hurt you, Annette, a hug is just a sign

18

of support and comfort. If I'm going to help you, you have to trust me completely. At the present time I'm the best friend you have.'

'Let me go.'

'No. Not until you relax. You're like hugging a tree. Relax, put your arms around me.'

'No.'

'Yes. No one can possibly creep up on you while I'm here. I'm quarter Cherokee. I hear better than a fox and I can see better than an owl.'

'Is that true?' she asked after a while.

'No, but it sounds comforting, doesn't it?' Through her tense body, he felt her have a little giggle.

Clay held her and stroked her matted hair. Relax, relax,' he whispered to her.

He held her for ten minutes, the tension slowly draining from her frail body. Eventually, he felt her arms go around him.

'There, that's not so bad, is it?' he asked.

'No,' she whispered, her head against his chest.

'Good,' Clay replied. 'Now, first, we have to get you fed and rested, then we'll talk, OK?'

'Yes.'

'You sit and I'll cook. I'm a damned good cook, even if I do say so myself.'

Clay sat Annette at the table while he cooked

steak and vegetables. They had a bottle of wine he had brought. For dessert they had apple-pie. Clay slipped some of the sleeping potion into Annette's coffee. By the time he had cleared the table and done the dishes, Annette was asleep, her head on her arms. He carried her to her bedroom and put her to bed.

Three

Annette awoke in a panic. She rushed to the kitchen and found a man in a white shirt and denim pants at the sink. He had his black hair tied back with a thong.

'What are you doing?' she asked.

'I'm cooking supper.'

'We just ate.'

Clay turned to her. 'You've been asleep for about twenty hours, it's nearly five o'clock.'

Annette went to pick up her rifle.

'Uh, uh,' Clay said. 'Remember, see like an owl and hear like a fox?'

She smiled. 'Sorry.' She looked around. 'Who did all the cleaning?'

'I did. If you don't mind me saying so, you look like shit and you're living like a pig.'

Annette hung her head in embarrassment.

Clay moved to her and lifted her head with his hand under her chin.

'Sorry, that wasn't very diplomatic. But look, people think you've gone mad, and if you live like this, you just give them more ammunition. Do you understand?'

'Yes.'

'Good. Now, there's hot water in the bath-house. You have a good bath and wash your hair. I've washed all the clothes I could find and I've ironed you a skirt and some shirts. You bathe, change, then in about two hours, we'll have a fine chicken-roast. It's one of your chickens, I'm afraid. I was on the way to the barn and he attacked me, so I shot him.'

When Annette emerged from the bath-house she found Clay sitting out in the sun.

'Better? ' he asked.

'Yes, thank you.'

Clay made her sit, then he took her hair-brush and brushed out her hair before plaiting it.

'How did you learn to do that?' she asked.

'Doing my grandmother's hair, originally. She's a full-blood Cherokee. I have a sister who is ten years younger than me. I used to do her hair. Before the war, anyway.'

'What happened?'

22

'My family live in Virginia. I fought for the Union, my brothers fought for the Confederacy. One of them lost half his leg, so I'm not real welcome at home, I'm afraid. Gran, Mother and Sis are always pleased to see me, but with Pa and my brothers it's not good. I've only been home twice since the war.'

After supper, Clay found Annette at the door, staring out into the night.

'Come and sit down,' he said to her.

Annette didn't move.

'I miscarried at about four months,' she said, barely audibly. 'I buried my baby there, under that old oak. I sometimes wonder if I could have loved a child conceived under those circumstances.'

Clay turned her to him and held her by her arms as tears rolled down her cheeks.

'You'd have loved your child, Annette, there's no doubt in my mind. You're a gentle, compassionate, loving person. What happened wasn't your or your baby's fault. Your baby would have been part of you, the very best part.'

Annette stood looking at Clay, then she started to cry; huge racking sobs that shook her body. Clay took her in his arms; there was no resistance now.

23

'You cry, Annette, you cry all you like.'

She cried for ten minutes, then she was quiet.

'Time for bed,' Clay whispered into her hair and led her to her bedroom. He left her while she got into bed. He went and poured some of the sleeping-potion into a small amount of coffee. 'Drink that,' he told her when he returned to her room.

'You drugging me?' she asked wanly.

'Just something to make you sleep.'

Annette drank then settled down into her bed. She held out her hand.

'Don't go, please?' she pleaded.

Clay sat on the edge of the bed.

'I'm here, don't you worry.'

Four

For the next few days, they just relaxed. They rode out and Annette showed Clay around her ranch. It was a fine bit of country, well-watered and well-grassed. There were quite a few cattle, mostly cows and two lots of calves, born since Mr McLean had been killed. Of course Annette hadn't been interested in doing ranch work.

By Thursday, Clay had been living with Annette for a week. She looked much healthier and wasn't as much on edge. Mid-morning, she rushed into the house and went for her rifle.

'Someone's coming!' she yelled frantically.

'Don't worry, I know who it is,' Clay told her after looking down the trail.

'Who is it?'

'It's the O'Days, the preacher and the undertaker. I arranged for them to come out.' Clay held her by her hands. 'Annette, I have to exhume your father's remains. Then, I thought, you might like to rebury him in your family plot.'

'You don't believe me, you don't believe me!' Annette yelled and tried to hit him.

Clay grabbed her by the arms.

'Listen to me, Annette, listen to me!' he yelled back. 'Look, if someone asked me what are the two greatest certainties in the world, I'd tell them that one is the sun rising in the east, the other is that Annette McLean is telling the truth. But I have to be able to prove it. Knowing it isn't enough. Do you understand?'

'Why do you believe me? You hardly know me.'

'Because I read your letter, Annette. I read the pain and despair in it. It's inconceivable to me that you could write such a letter if those things hadn't happened to you. I've read the doctor's report, and I know some things that you don't know.'

'Like what?' Annette asked doubtfully.

'Like, I know that the five men you named in your letter sold your cattle in Abilene. I know that three returned to Texas and the other two went to Kansas City. I know that I can make a case against these men and I know that I will.

There is something you must realize though, and it's this. I may have to say or do things you don't like, but always remember, it's so I can bring these men to justice. This is what I do, Annette, and I do it very well, all right?'

'Yes.'

Clay hugged her. 'Good. Incidentally, your cattle sold for sixteen dollars a head, so someone owes you thirty-five thousand, three hundred and forty-four dollars. We'll get that too. Now, let's go and greet your visitors.'

Annette restrained him. 'You're a lovely man, Clay,' she said softly.

Clay took her hand, he looked into her face, which even after a week, was beginning to glow with good health. It startled him to realize the depth of feeling that he had for this young woman.

'Thank you,' he replied. 'You have no idea how much I appreciate your saying that.'

The doctor and his wife were astounded at how well Annette looked. While Annette entertained the preacher and Mrs O'Day, the undertaker and his helper dug a grave alongside the grave of Annette's mother. While they did that, Clay and the doctor exhumed the body of James McLean.

James McLean lay in a shallow grave Annette

had obviously scraped out with her hands. Then she had covered him with stones. Clay was struck by the absolute despair that Annette must have felt as she laboured to cover her father, stone by stone.

The corpse was now just leathery skin, stretched over bone. James McLean's mouth was open, as if in one final scream. Or perhaps he was cursing his murderers. Clay removed his partly decomposed leather vest; there were two bullet holes in the back of it. When they inspected the skeleton, it was apparent that one bullet had smashed McLean's spine.

'At least he died instantly,' the doctor told Clay.

They buried James McLean next to his wife. Annette cried softly. Clay stood with his arm around her shoulders. Again Annette felt the despair she had felt when her father had been murdered. How could this have happened? Who had the right to destroy a family in this way? Her father had done nothing to deserve to die in this fashion, in his early forties. Whenever her determination wavered, she had only to think of the gentle man who had raised a daughter alone. This strengthened her resolve. And she had Clay. It startled her to realize the strength she drew just from being close to this man. She knew that together they could get justice.

After the funeral, Annette served her guests refreshments, then they all departed.

Five

In the morning, Annette was startled to find Clay wearing his black suit. His guns were on the kitchen table.

'Today we go to work,' he told her.

Annette was almost panic-stricken when Clay told her that she would be staying in town with the O'Days.

'I can't,' she protested.

'Yes, you can. You can't live out here like a hermit for the rest of your life. You have to start seeing your friends again.'

Annette gave a derisive laugh. 'Friends? I haven't seen anyone since this happened. You'd think that I did something terrible.'

'Well then, you'll stay with the O'Days and

you'll make all your so-called friends feel as bad as they should feel. The O'Days are your friends and so am I, that's a start.'

Annette gave him a rare smile. 'Yes, that's a great start.'

As Clay went to help her into the buggy, she paused.

'Clay, I want to go with you.'

'You sure?' he asked.

'Yes. When you arrest these men, I want them to know that I'm strong enough to stand up to them. I won't let what they did just fade away.'

Clay squeezed her arm. 'Good for you.'

Jack Hunt farmed somewhere on Cottonwood Creek, Annette informed him. They met a boy driving a cow and a calf along with a stick; he directed them. The place was very neat, the corn-crop about a foot high. Clay headed to the house. As he tied the horse to the hitch rail, a man came out of the barn, which was on the right of the house. He carried a rifle. Clay eased his revolver in its holster.

'Mr Hunt?' he enquired.

'Yeah, who're you?'

'My name's Clay Blake.' He reached out and gave his hand to Annette. 'I'm sure you remember this young lady.'

31

Jack Hunt looked at Annette. His face turned ashen and he dropped his rifle.

'Oh my God,' he gasped. 'I've been expecting you, Miss McLean.' He turned to Clay. 'You a gunfighter?' he asked.

'Sometimes, Mr Hunt. But actually, I'm a federal marshal. You're under arrest for, well, you know what you're under arrest for, don't you?'

'Yes.' He turned to Annette. 'I'm sorry, Miss McLean, I was drunk. I just can't control myself when I'm drinking. I'm sorry.'

Clay grabbed Jack Hunt by the shirt and stuck his revolver under his chin.

'You think being drunk excuses you, you bastard? You're lucky I am a marshal, because I'd kill you here and now if I wasn't.' Clay pushed him. 'Now, into the house.'

The house was as neat as the rest of the farm, which was surprising.

'Before we go, Mr Hunt,' Clay said, 'you owe Miss McLean seven thousand and sixty-nine dollars, near enough. Where is it?'

Jack Hunt went to the fireplace and removed a stone. He returned with a tin box.

'There's six thousand dollars in there. The rest went on this farm and just general spending.'

Clay handed Annette the money. In the box was the deed to the farm.

'You write?' Clay asked.

'Yes.'

'Good. Get some paper and write out a transfer of ownership of this farm to Miss McLean.'

'You can't,' Jack Hunt protested.

Clay cuffed him over the head.

'I can, you bastard. Why the hell do you think we're here? You think Miss Mclean is here to forgive you? She wants you dead, I want you dead, the only reason you're still alive is because I'm the law. You'd better get used to the idea that you're never coming back here, never. Now write.'

Jack Hunt started to write.

'I was drunk, can't you understand? I was drunk.'

'Well,' Clay said thoughtfully, 'perhaps a judge would see that as mitigating circumstances. I know that if you were to write a confession and I could tell the judge that you co-operated, you might get a break.'

'Clay, you can't,' Annette protested.

'Be quiet,' Clay told her sharply. He turned to Jack Hunt. 'One chance, Hunt. A full confession, or I push for a hanging.'

'All right,' Jack Hunt whispered.

Annette was aghast. Clay took her by the arm and marched her to the door.

'Remember what I told you, Annette, I'll do or say anything to get these bastards. With a confession we've got them, do you understand? We've got them.'

'But this one will get leniency, you as much as told him.'

Clay smiled. 'Did I say that? I don't remember.'

Annette smiled briefly and leant her head on his chest. 'I'm sorry, I shouldn't yell at you. I'm just not very trusting.'

'You yell at me all you like. On the way to town, how about we see the neighbours about farming your farm? Seems a shame to let that nice corn-crop go to waste.'

'That the farmer in you coming out?'

'Yes.'

Clay returned to the table and read Jack Hunt's confession.

'Best you say that you weren't coerced in any way.'

'What does that mean?'

'That you confessed voluntarily. Just write that on the bottom.' Jack did so.

They waited while Jack saddled his horse. When they were ready to leave, Clay held up his rifle in the buckskin scabbard.

'This is a Henry .44, Mr Hunt. If I can see you, I can shoot you. Try to run and that's exactly what I'll do, clear?'

'Yes, sir.'

Clay stopped in on the neighbours, the James family. Clay explained that Annette was now the owner of Hunt's farm. He asked Mr James, would he be interested in farming it. Mr James replied that he would like to buy it. Annette agreed to sell at whatever he thought was a fair price, payable however he liked.

Mrs James was a Mexican lady. Before Clay drove off , she approached Annette.

'*Señorita*, I am most happy to see you looking so well. We tried to take you food early on, but you shot at us. I prayed for you, that was the best I could do.'

Annette climbed down and hugged the black-haired lady.

'Thank you, Mrs James,' she said emotionally. 'I hope you'll forgive my behaviour. As you can see, your prayers were answered, God sent Marshal Blake to help me.'

They moved out for town. Annette quietly linked her arm through Clay's.

Clay and Annette escorted Jack Hunt to the jail.

'Lock him up,' Clay told the sheriff. When the sheriff returned from the cells, Clay showed him Jack Hunt's confession. The sheriff read it but didn't comment.

Two deputies returned just as the sheriff handed the confession back to Clay. Roy Wallace smirked at Annette.

'Well, look who's here,' he said derisively. 'Rape, rape,' he yelled in a high-pitched voice, then laughed at his own joke.

Clay sprang at him, he spun him around and slammed him face down across the desk.

'You think it's funny, you bastard? You think it's funny? Well, let's see just how funny it is.'

Clay pulled out his Bowie knife, stuck it in the top of the deputy's trousers, and slit his pants and long johns down to the crotch. He reached across and pulled out the deputy's revolver and jammed it between his buttocks. Roy Wallace screamed.

'Is it funny yet, Deputy?' Clay asked. 'Of course, you're not a young girl, being held down by four disgusting bastards who are laughing at you. But never mind, you wanted a demonstration of what happened, so now you're going to get it.'

Roy Wallace screamed hysterically as Clay

36

exerted pressure on the revolver.

'Stop!' the sheriff yelled. 'Stop, or by hell I'll shoot you.'

Clay cocked the revolver he was holding.

'Go ahead, Sheriff,' he said. 'See if you can shoot me before I blow this bastard's brains out. I'm at the right end.'

Annette stepped forward and put a hand on Clay's arm.

'Enough Clay, please?' she pleaded.

'You hear that, Deputy?' Clay asked the sobbing man. 'The young lady you like to make fun of has taken pity on you. Why couldn't you do the same for her? Or did it make you feel like a big man having someone to belittle?' Clay let the man go and dropped the hammer of the revolver. 'You disgust me, you really do,' Clay said to them all.

The deputy rolled off the desk, on to the floor.

'Incidentally,' Clay said, 'now you know why I'm here, I'll take Devenish and Watts in town on Saturday night. I'm sure they'll be in a saloon somewhere. Right, Sheriff?'

'Yeah, probably.'

'So, if they get wind of what's going to happen, I'll know it came from one of you. Then I'll arrest you all, for impeding an investigation. Clear?'

The sheriff and the other deputy replied: 'Yes.'

Clay jabbed Roy Wallace with his toe.

'Clear?'

'Yes.'

Clay took Annette by the arm and they headed for the door.

'You're an animal, Blake,' the sheriff said.

Clay turned back. 'Yes, Sheriff, I'm an animal. But I'm the one who's going to get this young lady justice. So stay out of my way, or you'll wind up in jail, too.'

On the street, Clay told Annette that he had to go to the telegraph office. Annette said that she would go to the bank and deposit her money.

'Will you be all right?' Clay asked.

'I've got to start sometime. Besides, John Atkins, who is one of the tellers, well, he was courting me before all this happened. He disappeared like everyone else, but we should still be friends, I suppose.'

'All right, off you go, I'll come and collect you.'

Clay watched her walk away. He wondered how much inner strength it was taking her to set out on her own for the first time.

Clay collected two messages and sent reports to his superiors. He was nearly to the bank when Annette almost collided with him. She was running and crying.

'What the hell happened?' Clay asked.

'I saw John, he asked me to invite him to supper, he said he'd be happy to stay the night.'

Clay took her hand and they returned to the bank.

'Which one?' he asked.

Annette pointed to a young man. Clay pushed his way through the customers, grabbed the clerk by the shirt-front, hauled him half-way across the counter, then punched him right in the face and sent him sprawling. Nimble as a cat, Clay jumped the counter and grabbed the prostrate man.

'You ever say anything like that to Annette again, I'll kill you, is that clear?'

'Yes,' the man mumbled.

Clay leapt the counter again, offered his arm to Annette and they walked out into the street. Clay could feel her looking at him.

'What?' he asked.

'You're a strange man, Marshal Blake,' she said with a smile.

Six

On Saturday afternoon Clay staked out the saloons on Main Street. When he returned to the O'Days he told them that the Circle D hands were drinking in the Lone Star saloon. After supper he told them: 'Time to go to work.'

Annette had become more and more worried as time wore on.

'Clay, I don't like this,' she said. 'Perhaps you'd better try to get some help.'

Clay went to his room and returned with his shotgun.

'Mr Greener is all the help I need,' he told her.

'Clay, this isn't a joke.'

Clay took her hand and squeezed it.

'Don't worry, Annette. They sent the Cherokee to do the job and it will get done. Now, do you want to come or stay here?' She wanted to go, of course.

They walked arm in arm to the Lone Star. It was easy to pick the men they wanted from all the drinkers. Watts wore black, and not many men wore their gun butt forward. Clay moved behind the two men and prodded them both in the back with his shotgun.

'Hey,' he said. Both men turned.

Clay held his small wallet in front of them.

'I'm Clay Blake, federal marshal.' He nodded towards Annette. 'You know who this lady is, so I'm sure you know why I'm here.'

Bud Devenish giggled.

'Hello, Annette, you look great.' To Clay he said, 'You've got nothin' on us, Marshal.'

'I've got enough to hang you, Buddy. Now drop your guns.'

In the blink of an eye, while Clay was talking to Bud, Billy Watts went for his guns. Without taking his eyes off Bud, Clay lifted his shotgun and shot Billy Watts in the chest. The impact drove Billy backwards against the bar and he slumped slowly to the floor.

'Want to try for two out of two, Buddy?' Clay asked.

Buddy sank to his knees beside his dead companion.

'My pa'll crucify you, Injun,' he said.

'If your father gets in the way, I'll arrest him too. Now stand up and remove your gun.'

There was a commotion behind them, and the sheriff and a deputy appeared.

'Shit,' the sheriff said. 'What happened?'

'What's it look like, Sheriff?' Clay asked.

'What happened, Joe?' the sheriff asked the barman. Joe told the sheriff what had happened, and assured him that Billy had gone for his guns.

'You didn't give him a chance,' the sheriff said.

'I wasn't interested in giving him a chance, Sheriff. He drew on a man holding a shotgun. What the hell do you think would be the result? Right, you,' Clay said to Bud. 'Off to jail.'

'Go get the old man, Jake,' Bud said to another rider, as he headed for the door.

They marched the surly Bud to jail.

'You won't hold me, Injun,' Bud shouted as Clay swung the door shut.

'Yes I will, Bud. Get used to it.'

After all the excitement of the evening, Clay escorted Annette to her bedroom door.

'Everything will be fine, don't you worry,' he assured her.

As he turned to leave, Annette restrained him.

'Clay, I wish that we could have met under

different circumstances,' she whispered softly.

Clay took her hand. 'Thank you, Annette. But young ladies like you don't meet men like me under normal circumstances.'

'Why do you say that?'

'Because when I go to a town, I go on business. People are pleased to see me because I'll fix whatever problem they have. But most of them don't like me, most of them don't trust me. They don't invite me home to supper, and they sure as hell don't introduce me to their daughters. I do the job and then they want me gone. That's how it is.'

'That's not right.'

'What's right has nothing to do with it. What happened to you isn't right, that's why I'm here. I didn't come to make friends, but I will make enemies.'

'Well, I like you, I trust you, and I would like to cook you supper. Tomorrow evening, all right?'

He smiled at her in the soft light of the lamp.

'Thank you, Annette, I'd like that very much.'

To Clay's surprise, she kissed him on the cheek.

'Goodnight,' she whispered.

'Goodnight,' he responded.

Seven

Mid-morning on the Monday, Clay was sitting on the O'Days' porch, reading some messages and reviewing his papers concerning Annette's case. He was approached by a distinguished-looking man, and a beautiful girl, who looked to be slightly older than Annette.

'I'm Colonel Devenish,' the man said. 'This is my daughter, Margot.'

'Just a moment,' Clay said and continued to read.

'Don't keep me waiting, boy,' the colonel said.

Clay finished reading, then sat back and observed his visitors; the girl watched him speculatively.

Eventually, Clay said, 'I'll make a deal with

you, Devenish. You don't call me boy, I won't call you Colonel.'

'Everyone calls me Colonel, Marshal,' the man answered derisively.

Clay picked up a piece of paper and read out loud: 'Clay, no such animal as a Colonel Devenish. Houston made everyone a Colonel. Signed, Andrews.'

The man was furious. 'I checked on you too, Blake. They call you the fixer, anything looks impossible they send you. So fixer, how do we fix this mess?'

'Well, I'll tell you, Mr Devenish, your son and his minder both owe Miss McLean seven thousand and sixty-nine dollars. First off, we fix that.'

'That's impossible.'

'No it's not, Mr Devenish. Your son and his companions sold the McLeans' herd in Abilene last summer. August fifth, to be exact.'

'Ridiculous!' Devenish yelled.

Clay slammed his hand on the table.

'No it's not!' he yelled back. 'Don't try to take me for a fool. Did your son go to Kansas last spring?'

'Yes, but . . .'

'Don't but me, Mr Devenish. Just take it for a fact that your son and four others stole the

McLeans' cattle, drove them to Abilene, then sold them. I'm sorry, but there's absolutely no doubt about it. You ever hanged rustlers, Mr Devenish?'

'Yes, I have. But look, Marshal, this is my son we're talking about.'

'I'm sure the rustlers you hanged had parents at one time or another, Mr Devenish.'

The man hung his head. Eventually he said, 'I'll go to the bank and get Bud's money. I can't guarantee that they'll give me Billy's money, though.'

Devenish hurried off. Margot still just stood, arms folded, leaning against the porch rail. She watched Clay with a slight smile on her face. Clay matched her stare.

'Well?' he asked at length.

'You're an interesting man, Marshal. The whole town is scared of you, even Father.'

'No one needs to be scared of me, Margot. As long as they haven't done anything wrong, of course.'

She smiled, pulled out a chair and sat.

'Ah, but most people have, Marshal. Haven't you?'

'No, not recently.'

'Well, you assaulted Deputy Wallace and killed Billy Watts. Don't you think that was wrong?'

'No. Wallace is a loud-mouthed oaf; he just got a demonstration of fear. As for Billy Watts, he was just stupid.'

'But you just gunned him down.'

'He drew on me and I killed him. I'm not interested in giving people a chance to kill me. When I go against someone it isn't for sport, it's life or death. I don't intend to be the one doing the dying. Sorry.'

Margot sat there silently, just watching him. 'Buddy's not quite right, you know,' she said.

'So I've been told. But that doesn't excuse what he did. Although I'm sure your father will realize that this is the only defence Buddy will have.'

'You don't like us much, do you?'

Clay smiled. 'Look, Margot, I'm sorry this is happening to you, I really am. This is one of the unfortunate side-effects of what I do. Families always get hurt. But Miss McLean has been hurt too, and it's my job to bring the people who hurt her to account. The fact that the father of one is a self-styled colonel and has everyone bluffed, and the fact that the person himself isn't marching to the same tune as the rest of us, is irrelevant.' Clay leant forward and placed his hand on the girl's. 'They did it, Margot, and I can prove it. Have absolutely no doubt about that. I'm sorry.'

Margot was silent for a while, studying the backs of her hands.

'Clay, would you like to join me for supper tonight?' she asked.

'Why? Do you think you can charm me into letting Buddy go?'

'Perhaps. But perhaps I just find you very interesting. Men like you are a rarity for me, I assure you.'

'Everyone's busting themselves to impress the colonel?'

Margot smiled. 'Something like that.'

'Well the answer's no. We're on opposing sides, you'd be demeaning yourself for nothing.'

Margot was about to speak when Annette burst through the door, carrying a tray.

'Clay, I baked a cake, I haven't done that for ages, so I brought you . . .' She stopped when she saw Clay had a visitor. 'I'm sorry, I. . . .'

Clay stood and took the tray. 'That's all right, Annette. You know Margot, I suppose?'

'Yes,' she whispered.

'Mr Devenish has gone to the bank. We hope that he should be back soon with some of your money.'

'I'll go inside then.'

Clay was about to follow her when Colonel

Devenish turned in at the gate. 'I got what money Bud had in his bank account, six thousand, two hundred dollars,' he said, threw it on the table. 'Billy had an account too, but they wouldn't give me that.'

'Don't worry, I'll get a court order.'

'So, is it fixed now?' the colonel asked. 'Will you let Bud go?'

'No, sir, I won't, never said I would.'

Colonel Devenish turned to his daughter.

'Come along, Margot,' he said. 'Incidentally, I've hired a lawyer to act for Bud. He said he'd drop by.'

'Let me guess. He'll plead that he was of unsound mind, right?'

'Yes.'

Clay smiled at Margot. 'Told you.'

Margot looked sad. 'You sure about supper?' she asked quietly.

'I'm sure.'

When Margot left, Clay hurried to the kitchen. He found Annette staring into space, hugging herself. 'You all right?' he asked with concern.

'Margot made you an irresistible offer,' she replied in return.

Clay took her in his arms. 'I think she made the offer, I didn't accept.'

'She usually gets her way.'

'Not this time.'

Annette was silent, her head against his chest, and when she looked up her eyes were shining. 'I'm not strong enough to do this alone, Clay,' she whispered. 'I thought I was, but I'm not.'

'Yes you are, but you're not on your own. I'll be with you every step of the way. The next few days will be hard for you, but we'll come out on top. Remember that.'

'I sometimes ask myself what's the point? We won't get them all.'

'Yes we will,' Clay replied firmly. 'The Murphy brothers bought a saloon in Kansas City. When we're finished here we're going there. We'll go to Galveston, then by boat to Norfolk, then by rail to Kansas City.'

'That seems a lot of trouble to go to.'

'Annette, I'd follow these men to the ends of the earth. I will get them, whether you come with me or not. Now, how about joining me for coffee and cake, before it all goes cold?'

Annette wiped her eyes, took Clay's hand, and they adjourned to the porch.

Later, Bud's lawyer, Richard Trewin, came by. Clay informed him that Judge Prescott would be in on the noon stage. He hoped to see the judge at about one o'clock. He suggested that Mr Trewin join them.

Judge Prescott was of similar build to Dr O'Day, except that he had a full head of grey hair. His passion for the law was exceeded only by his passion for his wife of twenty-five years, and their ten children. He always travelled with a prosecuting attorney, who was tall and spare, and sported a black beard. He reminded Clay of the late President Lincoln. He was aptly named, James Long. Clay had presented cases to Judge Prescott before. He always found him scrupulously fair, his rather benign features disguising a razor-sharp mind. James Long, too, was an extremely sharp man. Clay was happy to have them handling the case.

Both men greeted Clay and Annette effusively. The judge explained to Annette that she would have to wait in the hall until he had spoken to Clay and Richard Trewin. Clay got her a chair. 'If you want me, just knock,' he told her.

'Right, what have we got?' the judge asked, when everyone was seated.

Clay placed all his paperwork on the desk, then outlined the case as he saw it.

'Your honour, I would like to present all these

documents as the case against the defendants. I don't want Miss McLean to go through the trauma of telling her story in front of a jury.'

'Mr Trewin?' the judge asked.

'I should have the right to cross-examine her, your honour.'

'Marshal?'

'Your honour, in addition to an affidavit I have signed by the purchaser of the McLeans' cattle, in the presence of a judge, there is also a full confession, signed by Jack Hunt. These documents, along with a medical report, are our case.'

'Mr Trewin?'

'I must object, your honour.'

'Marshal?'

'Your honour, I have it on good authority that Mr Trewin is going to try to prove that Bud Devenish isn't playing with a full deck. This indicates to me that he concedes Bud is guilty but he's not responsible for his actions. Putting Miss McLean through a very harrowing experience isn't going to help his case at all. That's what I think, anyway.'

'Very well, gentlemen,' the judge said. 'If you give me half an hour to review the marshal's papers, I'll make a ruling.'

Clay stood in the hallway with Annette.

Richard Trewin stood alone. After half an hour, James Long ushered them back into the room.

'Mr Trewin,' the judge said, 'I have to agree with Marshal Blake. Forcing Miss McLean to relive her experience would be cruel in the extreme. I therefore rule that Marshal Blake's submission is acceptable as the case for the plaintiff.' The judge stood up. 'I'll see you at nine tomorrow morning, gentlemen.'

Annette now had to spend an hour with James Long. She had to relate the whole nightmare to him. When Clay was finally ushered into the room, Annette was dabbing at her eyes with a handkerchief. He hurried to the girl and helped her to her feet.

'You're a brave young lady,' James Long said to Annette as he showed them to the door. 'Don't you worry, I wish all the cases I try were as straight-forward as this one.'

It was natural now for Annette to walk with her arm linked through Clay's. It was as though she drew strength from her proximity to this man.

'Would you like to go out to supper, tonight?' Clay asked out of the blue.

'Why?'

'Why not? I'd like to take you out. I want everyone to wonder how a rather jaded part-Indian lawman can have such a beautiful young woman as a companion.'

'You're not jaded, Clay. You're quite remarkable, in fact. I'd love to go out with you, but I don't have anything nice to wear. I've had this dress since before the war.'

'Then we'll go shopping and I'll buy you a new outfit.'

'You don't have to. I have money.'

Clay looked at her and wondered if his eyes betrayed his feelings.

'I want to, Annette.'

She smiled radiantly. 'All right then, thank you.'

Eight

The courthouse was already packed when Clay
and Annette arrived. As they entered, the
Devenish family was just in front of them. Mrs
Devenish was a handsome, if somewhat frail-
looking, woman. She supported herself on
Margot's arm, rather than her husband's.

'All rise,' the sheriff said, as the judge entered
the room.

The judge sat and banged his gavel. 'This court
is in session,' he said.

The judge surveyed the large crowd before he
addressed the jury. He told them that due to the
very intimate details of part of the proceedings
they wouldn't hear Annette McLean testify.
Rather, they would hear evidence from the doctor,

and a confession from Jack Hunt. He looked at the prosecutor.

'Mr Long,' he said.

James Long called Clay as his first witness. Clay gave a detailed account of what he'd done since first being assigned the case.

'You never doubted that Annette McLean was telling the truth?' was the last question.

'No, sir,' Clay replied.

'Where were you when you were asked to look into this case, Marshal?' Richard Trewin asked.

'Chicago, Illinois.'

'Why did you come all this way? Did you know Miss McLean before this?'

'No, I didn't know Miss McLean. But I read the letter she sent to the governor. I couldn't imagine someone writing such a plea for help, unless what she said happened, had happened. It was quite easy then to ascertain that the McLeans' cattle had been sold by someone other than the McLeans. The men who sold the cattle matched the descriptions supplied by Miss McLean very accurately. After that it was easy.'

'You killed one of the alleged cattle thieves?'

'Yes, sir, he drew on me, I killed him.'

'Just like that?'

'Just like that.'

'Mr Trewin, the marshal isn't on trial here,' the judge said.

'Sorry, your honour. So, Marshal, it has never occurred to you that this could just be a story concocted by a spiteful or slightly deranged young woman?'

Clay smiled. 'No, sir, that never occurred to me.'

When Clay stepped down. James Long called Doctor O'Day.

'Doctor, you examined Annette McLean about two days after she says she was attacked?'

'Yes, sir.'

'Would you tell us what you found, please?'

The courtroom was silent as the doctor related the details of his examination of Annette.

'Miss McLean had been severely beaten. She had massive bruising to her ribcage and abdomen. I am of the opinion that she had several cracked ribs. She had also been sexually assaulted, and had suffered a severe loss of blood. So much so, that I confined her to bed in our home for a week. I can honestly say that I've never seen a woman so badly abused as Annette had been.'

James Long sat down.

'Mr Trewin?' the judge said.

'You have seen this type of abuse before, Doctor?' Richard Trewin asked.

'Unfortunately, yes.'

'But you only have Miss McLean's word about who did it?'

'Yes, but that's good enough for me.'

'You take a particular interest in Miss McLean?'

'I suppose so; she was the first baby I delivered here in El Paso. Then, when her mother died, I tried to help her father as much as I could. He was a good man and Annette is a fine young lady.'

'You take this much interest in all the children you've delivered?'

'You should know; I've delivered both of yours.'

Richard Trewin smiled. 'Yes I know. Have you had reason to doubt Miss McLean's sanity?'

'No, never,' the doctor replied firmly. 'I had grave concern for her future well-being, both physically and mentally. But since Marshal Blake arrived, I think she is well on the road to recovery.'

'Were you with the Marshal when he exhumed James McLean's body?'

'Yes.'

'Would you tell us what you found, please?'

'James McLean had been shot in the back,

twice. One shot severed his spine, he died instantly.'

'There's no possible way of knowing who shot him?'

'No.'

'So it could have been anyone? His daughter, for instance?'

'That's just ridiculous; no, it couldn't have been Annette.'

'In your opinion.'

'Yes, in my opinion.'

At the prosecutor's table, Annette was weeping silently. Clay put his arm around her and pulled her head on to his shoulder.

Next, James Long called Jack Hunt to the stand.

'Mr Hunt, you have made a confession in this matter?'

'Yes.'

James Long handed him a document. 'Would you read it to the jury, please?'

Jack Hunt paled noticeably. He turned to the judge, 'Do I have to?' he asked.

'Yes, Mr Hunt,' the judge replied.

Jack Hunt started to read his confession. Annette was crying so much that Clay put his hand over her ear, so that she couldn't hear.

Jack read; 'Me, Bud Devenish, Billy Watts, Ted and Mike Murphy, was hired by Mr McLean to round up his cattle and take them to Kansas. We was nearly ready to go, when one of the Murphys told the old man that we wanted more money. Mr McLean said no, and we said we wouldn't go. He was goin' to the house to get us our wages, when someone shot him. I don't remember who, because I'd been drinkin'.

'Annette came runnin' from the house. She was cryin' when she saw her pa, and she attacked one of the Murphys, Ted I think it was. He slapped her around somethin' awful and then we went to the house for supper. Annette threw hot coffee on Billy and he hit her some more.

'One of the Murphys tried to kiss her and she hit at him. He punched her hard in the stomach, then threw her face down across the table, and we all did what she said we did. Then we tied her to her bed and went to sleep.

'The next day, she begged us to let her bury her pa. We let her, but wouldn't let her have a shovel to do it. We made her do all the cookin' and some washin'. At night we did things to her again.

'We stayed at the ranch for four or five days. Annette was lookin' real sick, because the Murphys and Billy Watts sure liked to knock her about. Whenever she cried, they'd hit her. I didn't think she could take much more.

'When we decided to leave, Buddy reckoned that we should shoot Annette. Mike Murphy said no. He reckoned that someone might miss a good-lookin' girl like her, but if she told on us, who'd believe her? So we just left her. She looked so sick I didn't think she'd live, anyway.

'Then we hired a couple of 'breeds to help us drive the cattle to Kansas. We sold them, then me, Billy and Buddy came home. The Murphys stayed in Kansas, far as I know. Signed, Jack Hunt.'

The court was completely silent. Most of the jurymen were looking at the floor, as if shamed by what they had heard. Clay looked over his shoulder into the body of the court. Several women were dabbing at their eyes with handkerchiefs. Colonel Devenish looked as though he had shrunk. Mrs Devenish was being consoled by her daughter.

James Trewin broke the silence.

'No questions, your honour,' he said.

'Take him down, Sheriff,' the judge pronounced eventually.

James Long stood. 'That's all, your honour,' he said.

'Mr Trewin?' the judge asked.

James Trewin put Buddy on the stand. Through a lengthy questioning, Buddy's standard answer was, 'I don't know', or 'I don't remember'. It was obvious to all that he had been well-coached by his lawyer, or his father. Then it was James Long's turn.

'Mr Devenish, do you admit that you and your friends stole the McLeans' cattle?'

'I don't remember.'

'Come on Bud, you're not admitting to anything we don't know. You stole the cattle and took them to Abilene. Surely you remember going to Kansas.'

Bud picked at his fingernails. 'All right, we stole 'em. Old man McLean was dead, we'd spent weeks rounding 'em up, so we decided to sell 'em.'

'You all decided?'

'Yeah.'

Richard Trewin stood. 'Your honour . . .' he began.

'Be quiet, Mr Trewin,' the judge said sharply.

James Long continued; 'You said Mr McLean was dead. Who shot him?'

'I don't know. Someone.'

'Someone. Were you there when this someone shot him?'

'No. I don't remember.'

'Which is it? No, or you don't remember?'

'I don't remember.'

'You realize, of course, that Jack Hunt has said that you were all there when the shooting occurred?'

'Yeah, but he's a drunk. Who believes him? Besides that Injun.'

'Do you know what an accomplice is, Bud?'

'Yeah. He's your friend when you're doin' somethin'.'

Richard Trewin was on his feet, 'Your honour, he's putting words into Bud's mouth.'

'Sit down, Mr Trewin. Be careful, Mr Long.'

'Yes, your honour. Bud, Jack Hunt has confessed that you were all there when Mr McLean was killed. He said that there was an argument about money, and someone shot him. Is that right?'

Bud picked at his fingernails. 'Yeah, I suppose.'

'So someone shot him, but you don't remember who?'

'No.'

'Now, you know what Miss McLean alleges you did to her?'

'Yeah.'

'I suppose you don't remember that, even

63

though Jack Hunt said you all did it.'

'No, I don't remember.'

'But you do remember her being around?'

'Oh sure, she was comin' to Kansas as the cook, she's a good cook.'

'Was she present when her father was shot?'

'We were near the barn, she was in the house, I think. I remember her runnin' up. She sure can cry, I tell you.'

'What happened then?'

'We went to supper.'

'That's when you attacked Miss McLean?'

'I don't remember.'

'Well let me remind you that Jack Hunt has confessed that you all attacked her. Now, remember that word accomplice? That means if you were present when a crime was committed, and you did nothing to try to prevent that crime, you're as guilty as everyone else.'

Bud turned to the judge. 'That true?' he asked.

'Yes, Mr Devenish.'

'That ain't fair.'

'That's the law, Mr Devenish. Continue, Mr Long.'

'Thank you, your honour. Bud, do you know what mentally deficient means?'

'No.'

'It means you're a bit stupid. Are you stupid, Bud?'

'No I'm not!' Bud yelled. 'I'm as smart as anyone.'

The prosecutor smiled, 'I think so too, Bud. But your lawyer wants to prove you're stupid. He thinks that if he proves that you don't know what you're doing, the judge will let you go, but he won't. If you're guilty, you'll be sentenced to an asylum.'

Bud became very agitated. 'Pa? What's he sayin', Pa?'

'Address yourself to me, Mr Devenish,' the judge said.

'Is what he says true?'

'Yes it is.'

'That ain't fair.'

'So, Bud,' James Long continued, 'you were there, you're guilty, that's the law.'

'All right, all right, we did it to her. She was prancin' around showin' herself off. Pa says, you want somethin', you take it, boy, so we took her. She wasn't no fun, all she did was cry all the time. Pa? I want to go home now.'

Annette still sat with her head on Clay's shoulder, she had cried herself out.

'We've got them, baby,' Clay whispered to her.

Judge Prescott banged his gavel, 'We will adjourn now. Court will reconvene at half past one.'

The judge looked solemn when he seated himself. James Long summed up the case for the prosecution.

'These men have convicted themselves out of their own mouths,' he told the jury, then sat down.

Richard Trewin made much of the fact that everyone thought Bud wasn't too bright. Clay could see that this didn't impress the jury.

Before the judge spoke again, Clay was on his feet.

'May I address the court, your honour?'

'Yes, Marshal.'

'Thank you, your honour. Ladies and gentlemen,' he began. 'As you no doubt know, my name is Clay Blake, I'm a federal marshal. Some people call me Cherokee Blake, and, I'm told, my name instils fear into people. I don't know why; I'm just an ordinary man who does a thankless job.' He paused. 'Ladies and gentlemen, I'm thirty-five years old and I've been a lawman since I was nineteen, except for four years that I served in the Union Cavalry. In that time, I've seen things that no one ought to see. In the Wilderness, during the war, I saw dead men by the thousands. At Cemetery Ridge, we used bodies to build up the barricades. I've seen people hacked to death, burnt to death, shot, hanged, you name it, I've seen it. But if I was asked, what is the worst thing I've seen, I would say without doubt, it is how you people have treated Miss McLean. Good God above, what were you thinking of? Here is a young woman who was mercilessly attacked by five men, there is absolutely no doubt about that. But apart from Doctor O'Day and his wife, no one did anything. For more than a year she has been virtually without support. Mr Trewin tried to intimate that she's insane; it's a wonder she isn't.

'Your sheriff did nothing, because he thinks he needs Devenish support to get re-elected. His deputies asked Annette for a demonstration of what these men did to her. And yet, when I come to town, you all get indignant. I'm not a church-going man, ladies and gentlemen, but I'm sure a lot of you are. When you're in church next Sunday, singing hymns and talking about broth-erly love, if there truly is a God, He'll pull the building down on top of you. If I were you, I'd look to your God for forgiveness, because I'm sure Annette will never forgive you.'

Clay sat down. Annette had never seen him so angry, she squeezed his hand.

After a short pause the judge addressed the court.

'Miss McLean, I hope that you won't be upset by what I'm about to say. But I have to instruct the jury in law. In all good conscience, I have to tell them that if they find these men guilty, they cannot find them guilty of the murder of your father. The law is most specific. He was shot twice by five men. So, as a group, they can only be found guilty of complicity in the murder of your father. Gentlemen,' he said to the jury, 'you will retire now and consider your verdict.'

'Would you like a drink or something?' Clay asked Annette after the judge had left the court.

'No, thank you. Do you think they'll be out for long?'

'I doubt it.'

Clay was right. It was only about half an hour before the judge returned and the jury filed back in.

'Have you agreed on a verdict?' the judge asked.

A big man, whom Clay thought was the blacksmith, stood up.

'Yes your honour, we find them guilty of everything.'

Cherokee Blake

A loud din broke out in the courthouse. Annette cried uncontrollably. Clay held her to himself.

'We got them, baby,' he said. 'You cry all you like.'

The judge banged his gavel.

'Silence!' he shouted. 'Stand up, please,' he said to the defendants. 'Jack Hunt, Bud Devenish, you have been found guilty of the most heinous crime I have ever had to judge. For the theft of the McLean cattle, I sentence you to five years with hard labour, in the federal prison in Yuma, Arizona. For conspiracy in the murder of James McLean, I sentence you to twenty-five years, with hard labour. For your attack on Annette McLean, I sentence you to Yuma prison with hard labour. for the term of your natural lives.'

The court broke into uproar. Jack Hunt wept; Bud Devenish turned to his family.

'Pa? Sis? What's he mean?'

Annette cried on Clay's shoulder.

The judge banged his gavel. 'I'm not finished,' he said, and the court grew silent. He continued, 'I cannot comprehend the effect that this attack must have had on Miss McLean. I try but I can't. I suppose it's because I'm a man. So, I also sentence you both to twelve strokes of the lash.

Miss McLean, you may apply the lash yourself if you wish. Perhaps that will help to relieve the frustration you have felt up until now. If you don't wish to do it, Marshal, you will do it.'

Richard Trewin was instantly on his feet. 'I object, your honour.'

'I don't care, Mr Trewin, sit down.'

Clay stood up.

'Yes, Marshal?' the judge asked.

'Your honour, do you find the Murphy brothers guilty, in their absence?'

'Yes, I do.'

'Then I apply for arrest warrants for these men. I also apply for court orders to seize all assets of Bud Devenish, Billy Watts and the Murphy brothers.'

'So ordered, Marshal. Are you going after the Murphys?'

'Yes, your honour.'

'Good, good. Before I adjourn this court, I would like to say something. I wholeheartedly concur with what Marshal Blake had to say. How could you ignore this young woman's plight? I'm appalled, I really am, Sheriff. If I had the power, I would dismiss you. I have, however, read the town's statutes. I see that the town council has the power to dismiss you for incompetence. I'm dining with the mayor tonight, and I will suggest this to him most strongly. Remove the prisoners.' He banged his gavel. 'Court dismissed.'

The prisoners were led out, Bud yelling for his father. Annette still sat with her head on Clay's shoulder, she was near to exhaustion.

'You did it, baby,' Clay said into her hair.

'I couldn't have done it without you, Clay. I'll be eternally grateful.'

'It's my job, Annette.'

'No one is this dedicated to their job,' she said with a weak smile.

Clay smiled back, 'All right, I did it for you. Now we'll go to Kansas City and get the two Murphys.'

'You sure you want to?'

'Yes, I'm sure.' Clay stood up. 'Wait here until I see the judge, then you need to rest for a while.'

Annette waited with James Long until Clay got his warrants from the judge. She insisted that they leave by the front door.

The street outside the court-house was crowded. People stood silently, many looking sheepish. Clay could feel Annette as close to him as she could possibly be. Dr and Mrs O'Day were there; they started to clap and after a few beats everyone joined in.

71

The moment of euphoria was short-lived, however. Margot Devenish pushed her way through the crowd and rushed at Clay.

'Yuo bastard!' she screamed. 'You've destroyed our family!'

'Bud did that, Margot, not me.'

'It was you! You bastard!'

'Well, answer me one question, and if the answer is no, I'll break Bud out of jail and take his place myself. If you had been treated the same way as Annette had, would you want me to come and hunt down the men who did it?'

'That's not fair.'

Now Clay was angry. 'Answer the damn question, yes or no?' he yelled.

'Yes, all right? Yes.' Margot answered contritely.

'Then we have no more to talk about. If it had been my own brother who did this, I'd have hunted him down too.' Clay handed her a piece of paper. 'There is a warrant to seize any of Bud's assets, to make up the shortfall in his share of the cattle money. Out of respect for your parents, I'll let you go through his things. I'll give you two days. If you don't comply with this warrant, I'll come out myself and take everything Bud ever owned. Is that clear?'

Margot snatched the warrant. 'Yes, you bastard. I hope you rot in hell.' She stormed off.

On the way back to the O'Days' house, Clay and Annette stopped in at the saddler's. Clay bought a piece of leather about two inches wide and three feet long. He had the saddler cut it into four strips, but he left the last two inches in one piece. He also bought two pieces about four inches by two.

After supper, Clay and Annette sat on the porch swing and talked long into the night.

'What are you thinking about?' Clay asked after a lull in the conversation.

'Oh, I was just thinking, what happens to me once we get the Murphys. I'll be stuck in Kansas.'

'No, you won't, I'll bring you home.'

'Thank you.'

'That's all right. Actually, I was thinking that I might resign as a marshal. I thought perhaps you might give me a job as a cowhand. Other than that, I could buy a farm, run for sheriff, something. Then I'd be close, if you ever need me.'

Annette looked at him in the gloom. 'Clay, you can't disrupt your life, just to look after me.'

He laughed. 'My life, shit. Do you know what my life consists of? It consists of sitting in trains or stagecoaches for weeks at a time. It consists of going into towns and making enemies. My worldly goods consist of enough clothes to fill two carpetbags, enough guns to start a war, and about five thousand dollars in the bank. I don't have a family and I don't have friends. I don't own a home; shit, I don't even own a horse. Some life.'

'Don't talk like that,' Annette admonished. 'I'm sure there are hundreds of people you've helped, who consider you a friend. I do.'

'I'm sure they do, but I don't get to see them and I never get letters from them. I'm a memory, that's all. Don't get me wrong, I've enjoyed my life, I like what I do. When I started out it was a great adventure. But all the sadness and killing catches up with you. Do you know what my recurring dream is? I'm on a stagecoach for ever; when I finally get down, there are twenty men waiting and they kill me. They shoot me dead and just leave me there, and there's no one to be sad.'

Annette put a hand to his face. 'Oh, Clay, I'd be sad, all the people you've helped would be sad. Sometimes you can meet a person, and although you only know them for a short while, they have such an effect on you that you never forget them, never. That's how you affect people.'

'Thank you.'

They sat swinging until after midnight. Clay could tell by her breathing that Annette was asleep. He gently picked her up and took her to her room. He laid her on her bed and covered her up. As he turned to leave, she caught him by the hand.

'I'll never forget you, Clay,' she said.

Nine

It was after eight when Annette came to breakfast. She was very tense, Clay could tell.

'Are you going to do it?' he asked.

'Yes, I am. At least I think I am.'

'All right, have some breakfast, then we'll go. Doc, you coming?'

'Yes.'

While Annette had breakfast, Clay excused himself. He had attached the leather he had bought to a handle, and soaked it in water overnight. He tied several knots close to the end of each thong. He and Annette proceeded to the jail.

The sheriff was astounded to see Annette.

'She going to do it?' he asked.

'Yes. Bring Hunt out first.'

In the yard behind the jail, there was a tree. Clay had Jack Hunt remove his shirt and then put his arms around the tree; he tied Jack's wrists. Clay produced one of the small pieces of leather. 'Bite on that,' he told Jack.

Clay shook out the makeshift whip and handed it to Annette. It took her a while to get up the nerve to strike the first blow, then she struck and struck, her anger and frustration driving her almost to a frenzy. Clay had to step in after the twelve lashes.

'That's enough,' he told her. She was crying silently.

They cut Jack Hunt down, and the sheriff brought Bud out. He smiled insolently at them. Clay realized at that moment that although, at times, Bud seemed a bit simple, he was a cunning, evil man. Better his family thought he was stupid.

They dragged Bud to the tree and tied him. Clay offered him the piece of leather.

'She won't hurt me, Injun,' Bud said confidently.

'Yes, she will, Bud, and you'll scream. Let the whole town know what a tough man you are.'

Bud taunted Annette, telling her what it was

77

like to force himself on her. She stood as though she was made of stone, then she struck him, and yes, he screamed. She worked herself into a frenzy until she had hit Bud six times, then she collapsed to the ground, her breath coming in huge wracking sobs. Clay knelt beside her and held her to him.

'I can't, Clay, I'm sorry. I have no more anger left.'

'That's all right, sweetheart,' Clay told her. He held her for a few minutes then helped her up, 'Take her inside, would you please, Doc?' he asked.

When they were gone, Clay picked up the whip and moved to where Bud had sunk to his knees. 'How's it going, Bud?' he asked. 'Hurt, does it?'

'No more, please,' Bud pleaded.

'Only six to go, Buddy boy. These six are for what you've done to your family.'

Clay laid the lash on and Bud screamed, long and loud. At last it was finished.

'Cut him down,' Clay told the sheriff.

Inside, the doctor applied ointment to Bud's back. Clay hurried to Annette, 'You all right?' he asked.

'Yes, though I'm glad I did it.'

'Most people want to punish those who hurt them, Annette. I'm glad you did it, too.'

When the doctor had finished, he and Annette headed home. Clay had some things to do. As Clay was about to leave, the sheriff waylaid him.

'Look, Marshal,' he said, 'the mayor is going to recommend that I be fired. Would you try talking to him? I need this job.'

'No.'

'Come on, Clay, I have a family.'

'You have daughters?'

'Yes, one. She's ten.'

'Would you want her treated the way you bastards treated Annette?'

'No.'

'There's your answer then, Sheriff. I wouldn't piss on you if you were on fire.'

Before he left, Clay threw his makeshift whip into the burning potbellied stove.

Clay went to the bank and served them with a court order for Billy Watts's assets. He had a bank account containing $7,150. Clay transferred this money to Annette's account.

It was noon when he arrived back at the doctor's house. Annette was sitting on the swing-seat, waiting for him.

'Come with me,' she said excitedly. She led him to the rear of the house. 'Close your eyes,' she said and took his hand. 'Open,' she said eventually; he did so.

In the horse yard was a black gelding, about sixteen hands high, with a small star on his forehead.

'He's a beauty,' Clay said. 'Whose is he?'

'I bought him for you, now you own a horse.'

Clay was speechless. He went into the yard and patted the horse. He ran his hands over the animal's sleek black hide and stroked his soft muzzle. The horse turned to him and nuzzled Clay's hair, as if in welcome.

'Oh, Annette, he's absolutely beautiful. You shouldn't have spent your money on me, but I love him. Thank you.'

Annette clapped her hands in joy. 'Good. I knew you'd like him.' After a short pause, in which they both admired the horse, Annette said, 'Look, Clay, before we leave for Kansas, I'd like to spend a few days out at the ranch. Would that be all right?'

'Of course, give me a chance to ride my horse.'

Annette was also happy to inform him that she had hired a young man, who had a wife and two children, to stay on the ranch while she was away. When she returned, he would stay on as a hand.

'I feel like doing things now,' she told Clay.

'That's good.'

Ten

Annette wouldn't have admitted it, but the trial had taken a great deal of her strength, and the doctor ordered her to rest before she and Clay started on their trip to Kansas City. For two days, Annette just sat around and retired to bed early each evening.

Clay, too, used this time to recuperate. People probably didn't realize that this kind of job was very testing for lawmen. It took an exceptionally strong man to come into a town and enforce the law. Especially when, as in this case, he had to go against the most prominent family in the county.

It was nearly ten o'clock at night. Clay was sitting alone on the porch when he heard the pounding of hoofs. He'd heard this sound often enough to know that at this time of night galloping horses meant trouble. Sure enough, eight or nine riders, it was hard to count them in the dark, raced down the street to the doctor's house. The riders wore hoods. Clay dived in through the front door, just as a volley of shots tore into the front wall of the house, breaking two of the front windows. Clay rushed to Annette's room. She was just entering the hallway. He dragged her down on to the floor.

'Stay down!' he commanded.

Annette was almost hysterical. 'I knew they'd come, I knew!' she screamed.

Clay shook her vigorously. 'Stop!' he yelled. 'They're here for me, or to break Bud out of jail. Now you stay here. Doc!' He called to the doctor who was crawling up the hall. 'Keep the ladies here at the back of the house. I've got to go out.'

Annette protested vigorously, but Clay was adamant. He went to his room and got his revolvers and a shotgun. He gave one revolver to the doctor. 'Anyone except me comes through the door, you shoot him,' he ordered.

Staying in the shadows, Clay sprinted to the jail. He could hear the occasional shot and people yelling. When he was within sight of the jail, he could see the hooded riders milling around. He heard someone yell, 'Don't worry Bud, we'll get you out!' Then the voice said, 'Let's head back to the doctor's!'

The riders wheeled away from the jail. Clay stepped into the street, and, using his shotgun as a club, he knocked one of the riders from his horse. Before he could grab him, however, someone screamed. 'Pa!' A rider raced up and hauled the man up behind him before galloping away. Clay had the foresight to grab the horse and tie him to the rail outside the mercantile store. He crossed the street to the jail and hailed the jailer from a discreet distance. A gruff voice asked who it was.

'It's Clay Blake,' Clay yelled back.

'Come on in, real slow.'

The jailer was a grizzled old man who held a shotgun.

'You here on your own?' Clay asked.

'Yep.'

'You all right?'

'Yep.'

Clay inspected the prisoners. Bud was cocky.

'My friends'll get me out, Injun.'

'Not likely, Bud.' Clay turned to the jailer. 'What's your name?'

'Bill Oldfield.'

'Well, Bill, if anyone gets in, you shoot Bud, all right?'

'My pleasure. I was friends with James

McLean. What they did to Annette was terrible. And like everyone else, I did nothin' to help her. So if it's the last thing I ever do, Bud, I'll splatter you all over that cell. Then I'll die a happy man.'

Clay looked at Bud; he could see that Bud took the old man seriously.

Clay took the captured horse back to the doctor's and unsaddled him. In the house he found the O'Days and Annette huddled together in the parlour.

'They're gone,' he told them. Annette was nearly hysterical. Clay assured her that the riders weren't after her, they were just ruffians letting off steam.

'Don't worry, I'll fix it. Come on, back to bed.'

After breakfast the next day, Clay hired a buggy, tied the captured horse to the back and headed for the Circle D. When he was in sight of the ranch house, he let the horse he had caught go, then followed on at a leisurely pace. Clay reined in near the barn where several cowboys were standing in a group. One held the horse and was stroking him.

'Your horse?' Clay asked.

'Yeah, so what?'

'How's your chest?'

'What d'ya mean?'

'Where I hit you with my shotgun when I knocked you off the horse.'

'Don't know what you're talkin' about.'

Clay smiled. 'Who's your son?'

The man didn't answer, but he took a furtive glance at a lad of about eighteen who was in the group.

'What's your name, son?' Clay asked.

'Billy Andrews.'

'Well, Billy, you and your pa are under arrest. Who else was with you last night?'

The boy didn't answer.

'Oh well, there were eight or nine men, I'll take you all in. We'll see if facing ten years in jail helps your memories.'

The men all laughed. 'You think you can take us all?' the older Andrews asked.

Clay just smiled. 'Come here, son,' he said to Billy. 'Look at my shotgun, what do you see?'

The lad inspected Clay's shotgun.

'The triggers are tied back, Pa,' he said.

'That's right. My thumb is the only thing between you and dying. Shoot me, I'll kill most of you. So, let's get saddled up. It's a long ride back to town.'

Before the men moved, Margot and her mother hurried up.

'What's happening here?' Mrs Devenish asked.

'Your men raided the town last night, ma'am. I'm here to arrest them.'

'Why?' Mrs Devenish asked the men.

'We was goin' to break Bud out of jail, ma'am,' Billy answered.

'Are you mad?' This dignified woman almost screamed. 'Hasn't this been enough of a disaster without anyone else getting killed? Was anyone hurt?' she asked Clay.

'No, ma'am. There was some damage to the doctor's house, and Annette was very shaken. Other than that, nothing. All right boys, get saddled up.'

As they waited for the men, Mrs Devenish said, 'You've got a gall coming here, Marshal.'

Clay smiled ruefully. 'Ma'am, I understand how you feel, believe me. But this isn't my fault. I just clean up the mess. If this had happened to you or Margot, I'd have left no stone unturned to get the culprits, believe me.'

'So you blame me and my husband, I suppose.'

'No ma'am, I don't blame you. I can't explain to you why this has happened. I can't explain why someone from an obviously loving family goes off the rails. But Bud did. Now his family has to suffer the consequences. If there was anything I could say or do to stop your suffering, I would. But there's not, I'm sorry. So you blame me all you like, if that helps. Understand this, though, if your men try to break Bud out of jail, there will be killing. Make absolutely no mistake about that.'

Mrs Devenish seemed to wilt before Clay's eyes.

'I just need someone to tell me why, Marshal.'

'I know ma'am. That's the question I've been asked a million times. If you can ever find the answer, you'll make a fortune and save a lot of people a lot of heartbreak.'

The woman turned away. 'Don't come back here, Marshal.'

'If I have to I will, ma'am,' Clay answered.

Clay watched her walk away. 'If I take these men away, is there any men left here?' he asked Margot.

'Don't tell me you're worried about us,' she replied derisively.

'Yes, I am.'

'Well don't be. There are other men, they're with father. They'll be back soon. I suggest you be gone by then.'

'Soon as these boys are ready, Margot.'

She turned and walked away.

It was mid-afternoon when Clay and his prisoners arrived back in town. People stood on the
sidewalk and watched as the little procession
passed by. They turned into the livery stables and
the men left their horses. When they all walked
out into the street, there were a dozen or so men
all lined up in front of them.

'Don't you move,' Clay said to his prisoners. To
the other men he said, 'What do you want?'

'You ain't puttin' them in jail, 'breed,' one large,
scruffy-looking cowboy said.

'Why is that?' Clay asked.

'Because it ain't right. You can't just come in
here and do as you like.'

'I'm here to enforce the law, mister, and you're
breaking it. So before you do something real
stupid, I'll give you a chance to walk away.'

The man grinned evilly and reached for his
gun. Clay swung his shotgun tip and jammed it
under the man's chin. 'Look at the triggers,
mister. Tell your friends what you see.'

'The triggers are tied back,' the man gasped.

'That's right. So if anyone shoots me, I'll drop
the hammers and I'll blow your head right off.
Now, the rest of you, go away. If you're still here

in ten seconds, I'll arrest you all for impeding me in the performance of my duty.'

The men slowly drifted away.

Clay followed his prisoners to the jail.

'Lock them up,' he told the sheriff.

'You're not serious,' the sheriff said.

'Yes I am.'

'You can't do this. These men were just concerned for their friend.'

'These men shot at people. These men damaged private property. These men could have killed someone. Good thing they didn't. Because if they had, you would have had to arrest them. You would have had to enforce the law. And we all know how good you are at that.'

'Well I'm not watching them.'

'That's a relief. I'd rather have Mr Oldfield watch them. At least I'll know they'll still be here in the morning.'

Eleven

In the morning Clay paraded his prisoners before Judge Prescott.

'What are the charges, Marshal?' he asked.

'Riotous behaviour, destruction of property, and attempted murder, your honour,' Clay replied.

The cowboys all burst out laughing.

'Who the hell did we try to murder, 'breed?' Andrews senior asked.

'Me,' Clay replied.

Bob Andrews could see that Clay was serious.

'Your honour, we was just lettin' off steam. What's happenin' to Bud ain't right.'

'Mr Devenish was found guilty by a jury of his peers, Mr Andrews.'

'Well, yeah. But everyone knows he ain't quite right. Besides, he wouldn't do such a thing.'

'For God's sake, Mr Andrews, he confessed. Do you think he did that just to make everyone's job easier?'

'No, sir.'

'At least, we agree on that, Now, Marshal, tell me the story please.'

Clay related the events of two nights previous.

'You sure it's these men?' the judge asked.

Clay told the judge about knocking the man from his horse, and that the horse had led him back to the Circle D.

'He your horse, Mr Andrews?' the judge asked.

'Yeah, but anyone could have taken him.'

'Remove your shirt, Mr Andrews,' Clay asked.

'No.'

'Do it,' the judge said.

Grudgingly, the man removed his shirt. His chest was badly bruised.

'Your horse, your son, and you are badly bruised. I find the case proven, Mr Andrews. I sentence you all to ten years in Yuma prison.'

'You can't!' Andrews screamed.

'I can Mr Andrews. The attempted murder of a federal marshal is a very serious crime. Quite apart from the fact that Clay is a close personal friend of mine. Everyone has to pay for their actions, sir. Bud Devenish, now you.'

'But what about the boy? You can't send him to prison.'

'Don't worry,' Clay interjected. 'I'll make sure he's in a cell with some disgusting bastard who will treat him like Bud and his friends treated Annette. If you're good, I'll get you the cell next door, then you can listen to him scream. Hell, he'll probably live for six months.'

'You can't, you can't,' Andrews sobbed.

Clay grabbed the man by the shirt. 'I can if I wish, mister. Now you know just how seriously I take my job. You're going crazy thinking what could happen to your son. What about what happened to Annette? Doesn't that upset you? It should. It damn well upset me, and I've seen things I couldn't even describe to you. Bud and his friends are guilty, believe it.'

'What do you want to do, Marshal?' the judge enquired.

'Let them go, Judge. Make them pay for all the damage they did, and make them apologize to everyone in the town today, before they go back to the ranch.'

'So ordered. You men are very lucky. Next time, you go to jail. Now get out. Marshal, I need to talk to you for a moment, please.'

When Clay walked out into the street, another

crowd had gathered. Not all of them were antagonistic this time, however. The mayor, who ran the general store, thanked him on behalf of the whole town. Margot Devenish, accompanied by two other cowboys, was sitting on her horse watching the proceedings.

'Can we talk?' she asked rather sheepishly.

'Sure,' Clay replied and helped her down.

Margot told Clay that she had brought whatever money she had been able to find amongst her brother's and Billy Watts's personal belongings. $175 from Billy and $322 from Bud. 'Clay, I'm sorry for how I spoke to you. I know this isn't your fault,' she said bashfully.

'Don't worry about it, Margot, people need someone to yell at, at a time like this. Can I ask you, have you and your parents seen Bud yet?'

'Yes. All he did was yell at us. He blames father for this mess. He thinks father should have been able to buy him out of trouble. He couldn't have though, could he?'

'No.'

'What did you want to talk about?'

'I was going to tell you that the marshals who take the prisoners to Yuma will be here soon. Don't try to be here and don't let your parents be here. Don't make things any harder for your-

94

Cherokee Blake

selves than they already are.'

'Thank you. Clay, I'd still like to have supper with you some time.'

'I can't, Margot. I'm sorry.'

Margot smiled rather wistfully and walked away.

At the rear of the assembled people, Clay found Annette, clutching a handbag and trying to look inconspicuous.

'What are you doing here?' he asked, with concern.

'I thought you might need some help.'

'You got a gun in your bag?'

'Yes,' she whispered.

Clay smiled, 'Thank you,' he said as he offered her his arm. 'You won't need to worry after tomorrow. According to the judge, the caravan to Yuma will be here at sun-up.'

'What's that?'

'It's the marshals who take the prisoners to Yuma prison.'

'Oh, God,' Annette said.

Clay was at the jail first thing to see his prisoners safely into the hands of the marshals. The caravan consisted of two wagons and a dozen heavily armed deputies. The marshal in charge

95

was Tom Hodge, a long-time friend of Clay's, and a veteran of years on the caravan. He had never lost a prisoner, although he had shot several over the years. Bud didn't have anything to say as he was pushed into one of the wagons. Jack Hunt cried.

'Have a long life, Bud,' Clay said as the wagons began to roll.

Clay and Annette spent two days at the ranch. The weather was perfect and Annette seemed to have regained her enthusiasm for life in general. Only once did Clay find her staring out at the old oak tree. He put his arm around her shoulders.

'Don't do this to yourself, please?' he asked.

'I'm all right. Let's go for a ride,' she replied.

Twelve

The coach trip to Galveston was uneventful for Clay. For Annette, it was the beginning of a great adventure, never having been away from El Paso. They went via Odessa, San Antonio, Houston, and numerous way stations in between. They were held up by high water at the crossing on the Pecos river. Annette insisted on seeing everything there was to see in every town. In Houston they attended the theatre. Clay was content to do whatever Annette wanted to do, just as long as she agreed to staying and eating in the best hotels he could find. They spent a day and a night in Galveston, before boarding a ship for Norfolk.

The boat-trip was, for Annette, quite overwhelming. For Clay, it was good if the weather was nice, as he was prone to seasickness. They put in at New Orleans, Louisiana, then Charleston in North Carolina. In each of the towns they spent the days seeing all the sights, their nights were spent dining in the best hotels.

The run up from Charleston to Norfolk was perfect. Annette liked to spend all her time on deck, in the wind and spray. Clay stood with her; the transformation from the girl he had first met was staggering.

Shortly after retiring one night, Clay heard a soft knocking on Annette's door, which was just across the gangway from his cabin. He pulled on his pants, got a gun and gently opened his door. The first officer, a young man of about twenty-five, whom Clay assumed was the captain's son, having the same surname, was there. He asked Annette if she would like a turn around the deck, it was such a lovely night. She answered, 'No.'

The young man grabbed her by the arm. 'Oh come on,' he said. 'That old Indian can't be much fun. You should be with someone your own age.'

'Clay is the best friend I have in the whole world,' Annette replied. 'Now let me go!' She was starting to get hysterical.

Clay stuck his revolver near the younger man's ear and cocked it.

'Let her go,' he whispered in the other ear.

The officer let Annette go and looked at Clay.

'You just made a big mistake, Indian,' he said. To Annette he said, 'I've changed my mind, goodnight.'

'You all right?' Clay asked as they watched the first officer walk away.

'Yes, thank you,' Annette replied.

She couldn't take her eyes off Clay; he was very powerfully built, something she had never realized before. On one shoulder and on his lower left ribcage there were circular scars. She automatically reached out and touched the one on his ribs.

'Bullet wounds,' he told her. 'Well, goodnight.' He went back into his cabin.

A short time later there was knocking on Clay's door. It was Annette, wrapped in a blanket.

'Can I come in?' she asked.

Clay stood aside and let her enter; she sat on the bed while he hastily put on a shirt.

'He frightened me a bit,' she told him sheepishly.

'Don't worry, get into bed.'

She did so. Clay sat on the edge of the bed and they talked until she finally dozed off. Clay sat and watched her. *He frightened me a bit*, she had said. If only you knew what I'm thinking, you'd sure be frightened of me, Clay thought. He wrapped himself in a blanket and lay on the floor, his head on a carpet-bag. Sleep was a long time coming.

When Clay woke, Annette was propped up on an elbow watching him, with just the hint of a smile on her face.

'I'm sorry I took your bed,' she said.

'Don't worry, but we'd better get you back to your cabin, without anyone seeing you.'

'Why?' she asked completely innocently.

'Because a young lady doesn't spend the night in a man's room, Annette.'

'Oh,' she answered and laughed sheepishly.

Clay opened both cabin doors. 'Coast is clear,' he told her.

She hesitated. 'Clay, you don't mind that I depend on you so, do you?'

'No, I don't mind in the least. Now get dressed, I'll call for you in half an hour.'

After breakfast, Blake and Annette were strolling on deck, when they were approached by Captain Young and the first officer.

'Mr Blake, Mr Young tells me you threatened him with a gun. Explain yourself, please.'

Clay looked at the first officer, who looked very smug.

'I didn't threaten him, Captain. I had a gun and I told him to let Miss McLean go. Captain, I'm a federal marshal, and Miss McLean is under my protection. That means no one will harass her, or assault her, no one.'

'I'm the law on this ship, Mr Blake, not you.'

'Fair enough, Captain. In my bags I have several warrants signed by a federal judge. I'll go and get one and fill it out in Mr Young's name. You are duty-bound to honour it, by putting Mr Young in detention, so that I can arrest him when we dock, and I will. It's not much of a charge but I'll find a judge who'll give him a fine if nothing else. Won't look good on his record.'

'I just held her by the arm, Pa,' the young man said.

The captain turned on him. 'On this ship I'm Captain, Mr Young, not Pa.' He turned to Annette. 'Is what Mr Blake says true, miss?'

'Yes, Captain.'

'Then I apologize, miss.' The captain turned to his son, 'Confine yourself to your quarters until I come and get you.'

'Yes, Captain. I apologize, Miss McLean.'

They all watched the young man walk away. 'Children,' the captain said. To Annette he said, 'Is there anything I can do to make your voyage

101

more enjoyable, Miss McLean?'

'Captain, this is the most exciting experience of my life. But yes, there is something. I'd like to climb into the rigging.'

Both men were dumbfounded. 'You couldn't climb in that dress, miss,' the captain said.

'I have a split riding-skirt. Please?'

The captain laughed. 'Mr Josiah,' he said to a huge Negro sailor who was coiling rope nearby. 'You and Mr Moore rope yourself to Miss McLean and take her to the crow's nest, if you please.'

Mr Josiah smiled and touched his forehead, 'Aye aye, Captain. Best I get her some canvas shoes to wear.'

Annette kissed the captain on the cheek and ran to change.

'You coming, Clay?' she asked as the two sailors roped her to themselves.

'Not on your life,' he told her, smiling at her enthusiasm.

Most of the passengers and crew assembled to watch. They had hardly started climbing, when someone said, 'Three to one she doesn't make it.'

'Will you take a hundred dollars?' Clay asked.

He certainly would.

In a frenzy of betting, Clay wagered $300 on Annette. The captain bet $100, Clay noticed.

Everyone craned their necks to watch the three people climb the rigging. The sailors didn't have to help at all, they just kept abreast of the slip of a girl. It seemed to take for ever, but they did make it. Annette climbed into the look-out, she waved frantically and yelled something that nobody could hear.

In twenty minutes, the three were down again. Annette jumped from the railing into Clay's arms.

'You're crazy,' he told her as he held her.

To his surprise, she kissed him lightly on the lips, 'You should have come, it was marvellous. You can see the land.'

'I don't want to see the land, not from up there. Besides, I was too busy betting on you.'

'Really? How much did we win?'

'*We* didn't win anything. *I* won nine hundred dollars.'

Annette looked disappointed, so Clay whirled her around.

'I suppose I can share it with you. After all, you did the climbing.'

They returned to the group of watchers. 'Settling time, gentlemen,' Clay said.

Two paid up grudgingly, the third said, 'Double or nothing, Indian.'

103

Clay smiled, 'I don't think so. Three hundred dollars please.'

'Pay up, Mr Jarvis,' the captain said, when the man made no move to do so.

Jarvis paid Clay and stormed off. The captain invited Annette and Clay to dine at his table that evening, as it was their last night at sea.

They sat in Annette's cabin and divided up their money.

'I'm rich beyond all expectations,' Annette said, then she was sad. 'Father had such plans. He used to say, "If we can just hold out until after the war". God.' Clay squeezed her hand. 'Clay,' she continued, 'You don't think it was all my fault, do you? Bud said that I was showing off, did that cause the whole thing?'

'No, and don't you think like that. You're a beautiful young woman and you were excited about the future. That's not a crime. If you wish to prance around, as Bud said, that's your right. You fell in with evil men. There was nothing you could do about that.'

'I've often wondered why they didn't just kill me.'

'Because they knew that it would be your word against theirs. It's a man's world, I'm sorry to say, Annette. I sometimes wonder how often this sort of thing happens and doesn't get reported. Quite often I'd say. Fortunately, you did everything right. You saw the doctor, you embarrassed yourself by reporting it to the sheriff, but that gave me something to go on. Other than that, I'd have got them for rustling, murder maybe, but for what they did to you? Nothing.'

'But you said you always believed me.'

'I did, right from the moment I read your letter. But I have to be able to prove it. I'd like a dollar for every case I've looked into, where I knew someone was guilty. I knew it, but I couldn't prove it.'

Annette held Clay's hand in both of hers. 'I'll bet that you wouldn't have much.'

Clay smiled. 'Perhaps not, but even one dollar is too much. Now, no more sadness. I'm going to have a lie-down; I didn't get much sleep last night. Then, tonight, you can wear your best dress when we dine with the captain, and everyone will think I'm the luckiest man in the world.'

Thirteen

As the train drew closer to Kansas City, Annette grew more pensive. They arrived shortly before noon, and booked into the Alma Hotel.

As they were eating lunch, they were confronted by the sheriff and three deputies. The sheriff was a tall, gaunt man, with a grey walrus moustache. The deputies all carried rifles. Annette was quite unnerved.

'Well, well,' the sheriff said, and turned to his deputies. 'You sure were right, Joe, when you said a bad lookin' bastard got off the train, with a beautiful young woman. Any of you have any idea who this is?'

'No, sir,' the deputies all answered.

'You all want to be good lawmen, right?'

'Yes, sir,' they all answered again.

'Well, there's good and then there's the best, and this is him, this is Cherokee Blake.' The sheriff's face broke into a smile and he held out his hand. 'Hello, Clay,' he said in welcome.

'Hello, Ned,' Clay said and shook the outstretched hand. He introduced Annette and asked the sheriff to sit.

'Go get some dinner, boys,' the sheriff said to his deputies. 'If there's one thing Clay hates it's someone interrupting his meal. So, you go eat and I'll sit here. I'll find out why the Fixer is here, eventually.'

Clay laughed and continued to eat.

They all had coffee. Clay and Sheriff Amos had apple-pie also. Clay enquired after the sheriff's family.

'Molly's started a dress-shop. We hope to be able to put something aside for our retirement. But Lizzie, 'she's our oldest,' Amos explained to Annette, she wants to be a doctor, can you believe that? So that will cost the earth. If she can get into a medical school, of course. She's in New York, now.'

'That would be marvellous, Ned,' Clay said. 'I'm sure there's a big need for lady doctors. If you like, when we finish our business here, we'll go to

107

Cherokee Blake

New York. I'm sure if I stick my shotgun up someone's nose, she'll get in somewhere.'

The sheriff smiled. 'No need for that, at the moment, thanks. Lizzie's met another girl who wants to be a doctor, too. Her father is some sort of tycoon and has lots of influence. He'll get things moving for them. Now, you mentioned business, Clay.'

Clay explained the purpose of their trip to Kansas City. He produced his arrest and seizure warrants.

'These Murphy brothers, don't know them,' the sheriff told them.

'You know them as Ted and Mike Smith, they own the Deuces Wild saloon.'

'Yeah, I know them, don't like them, either. Talk is, that Mike has beaten up some of the girls who work for them. Had no complaints though. Apparently Ted paid them off. So, what do you want to do?'

'I think I'll get Mr Greener, then we'll go and arrest them. How does that sound?'

The sheriff stood up. 'Sounds good to me.'

Clay collected his shotgun, and the three of them walked to the Deuces Wild. The sheriff asked the barman where the brothers were. 'Upstairs in the office,' he was told.

They went upstairs. The sheriff knocked on the office door. Clay told Annette to stay in the hall for a moment. When Clay and Sheriff Amos entered the office, the brothers were sitting at a desk. Clay didn't like them. They both had florid complexions and were running to fat, but they both looked mean. The sheriff introduced Clay as a federal marshal.

'So?' one brother asked.

Clay dropped his warrants on the desk. To give them their due, they weren't fazed at all.

'That ain't us,' one of them said. Clay thought it was Ted.

Clay went to the door and ushered Annette in.

'This them?' he asked.

'Yes,' she whispered.

'Well, boys,' Clay said, 'you're under arrest. Also, there's a warrant for seizure of all your assets. So open up the safe and let's see what Annette owns.'

The brothers argued long and loud, to no avail. The sheriff, who was growing tired of all the talk, drew his six-gun, stuck it in one brother's ear and yelled, 'Open the damned safe!' He stood behind Ted, as he obeyed. 'Don't come out with a gun, Ted,' he said.

Ted brought out a metal cash box.

'There a gun in there?' Ned asked.

'No,' Ted replied, in a surly fashion.

Ted threw papers and money on to the desk. Clay saw Ted look at his brother, and his eyes momentarily flickered to the rifle rack on the wall.

'Gun!' Clay yelled, as Ted brought a small revolver out of the metal box.

They all fired in unison. Annette screamed. Sheriff Amos shot Ted, from point-blank range. Clay shot Mike, just as he was reaching for a rifle on the wall. Then he went down, himself.

'Shit, Ned,' Clay said. He was holding his side and blood was seeping through his fingers.

Annette fell to her knees, holding Clay and crying.

'I'm all right,' he told her. 'Think he shot me through that old wound.'

'Don't make jokes,' Annette said through her tears.

'Hell, Clay, I'm sorry,' the sheriff said. 'The gun must've been in the lid.'

'Forget it, are they dead?'

'Yep, dead as they can be.'

Men with guns started to pour into the room.

'What the hell?' someone asked.

'Get out!' the sheriff ordered. 'Someone go get

the doctor and undertaker.'

'Before you go,' Clay said. 'I'm a federal marshal. I was here to arrest your bosses. They were sentenced to life in prison in their absence. Why is no concern of yours. I also have a warrant to seize all their assets on behalf of this young lady. So meet your new employer, Miss Annette McLean.'

'This right?' someone asked the sheriff.

'Yes,' he replied.

The doctor and undertaker arrived. Clay had been hit just a glancing wound under the old wound.

'You'll live,' the taciturn doctor told him.

'I'll nurse him,' Annette announced.

Apparently, the Murphy brothers didn't believe in banks. In the safe there was in excess of $20,000. In the metal box there was more money, and the deeds to the saloon, which they owned freehold.

'What happens to all this?' Annette asked.

'It's all yours,' Clay replied. 'All their assets were forfeited. They profited from your money, Annette. Now you're richer than you were before.'

*

Annette helped Clay back to their hotel, and insisted that he get into bed. He gave in to her demands. She sat on the edge of the bed, and broke into tears again.

'If anything should happen to you, I'd die,' she mumbled.

Clay sat up and took her in his arms, 'I'll be fine, sweetheart. Look, there's a few things to talk about. I don't suppose you want to stay here and run a saloon, so what will you do?'

'Sell, I suppose. Have you any idea how much it's worth?'

'Well, I enquired when I was here before. Fifty thousand dollars seems to be around the mark.'

Annette was absolutely speechless. It gave Clay a chance to bring up something else that had been on his mind.

'By the way, I'd like to go to Richmond, to visit my family before we go back to Texas. Would you like to come with me?'

'Yes, I would. Are you sure you still want to be a cowboy?'

'Yes.'

'Clay,' she said nervously. 'Don't take this the wrong way, but why on earth do you want to be a cowhand? You could be anything.'

Clay hugged her. 'Thank you, but I want to be a cowhand.'

'Well, for now, you just lie back. I'm going to spoil you rotten.'

Fourteen

For three days Annette nursed Clay. Molly Amos, the sheriff's wife, came to visit, and she and Annette became friends instantly. It was evident to Clay that Annette had told Molly what had happened to her. He hoped that being able to discuss it with a woman would help her recover from the experience.

Several rather wealthy-looking men came to enquire about buying the Deuces Wild. On the third day, Richard Marks and his wife, Doreen, came to enquire. Richard was a barman in the saloon and his wife was in charge of catering. They had about nine thousand dollars.

'Can I talk to you in private?' Clay asked Annette.

'Yes.'

The Markses waited in the hall.

'Annette, why don't you consider selling a half-share to these people? Then you'd have the opportunity of making a hell of a lot of money over the next six or seven years, until the railroad reaches Texas.'

'You think so?' she asked doubtfully.

'Well, yes. Look at the Murphys. They started with about fifteen thousand dollars. In just over a year they owned a saloon worth fifty thousand dollars, and had twenty thousand dollars in cash. And by the look of them, they'd been living high on the hog.'

Annette paced around nervously.

'You're right. But how can I keep a watch on my interests from a thousand miles away?'

'Employ Molly as your agent, she's a very smart lady. The money would certainly be handy with Lizzie in medical school. You, of all people, must see the need for lady doctors.'

'Yes, yes,' Annette said. She went to the door and asked the Markses in. She told them she would sell them a half-share for twenty-five thousand dollars.

'There are conditions,' she told them with a new-found air of confidence. 'None of the ladies who work in our saloon are whores. You'll pay them a reasonable wage, and they can keep all the tips they get. Also, Molly Amos is going to be my representative.'

The Markses were ecstatic. They were full of plans to make the Deuces Wild a high-class saloon and gambling-house. Molly Amos was only too happy to be involved.

Clay and Annette left for Richmond on a Friday. At the station, Annette gave Ned and Molly an envelope containing money. 'I want to help with your daughter's education,' she explained.

When they protested, Annette was as forceful as they. 'I insist,' she told them.

Ned and Molly opened the envelope, when they got home. It contained four thousand dollars.

Fifteen

Clay and Annette arrived at the Blake farm in the mid afternoon. As they drove their rented buggy up to the house, Annette could see two women working in a garden. As Clay climbed down, the younger woman started to run towards them calling, 'Clay, Clay.' To Annette's surprise, she was quite fair. She threw herself into Clay's arms and he whirled her around.

The young woman was introduced as Judith, Clay's sister. By now, Clay's mother had arrived. She was darker-skinned than Judith, but not as dark as Clay. An old woman with a walking-stick emerged from the house. Although her hair was now grey, it was obvious that Clay got his looks from her. Clay approached her almost reverently, as the others watched. They stood and looked at each other for a while. The old woman touched Clay on the cheek and spoke in a language that Annette couldn't understand. Then Clay hugged her for several minutes.

Eventually, he took the old woman by the hand and led her to where Annette stood with the others.

'Annette, this is my grandmother, Moon,' Clay told her.

The old lady spoke to Annette in what she assumed was Cherokee.

'She says she welcomes you, and you are very beautiful,' Clay told her. 'Grandma speaks perfect English,' he continued. 'She just uses the old tongue to see if I remember.' The old lady smiled and slapped him on the arm.

Two men emerged from the barn. One was introduced as Peter Jameson, Judith's husband. The other was Clay's father. Peter was warm and friendly, the father quite belligerent.

'You dragging your woman around with you, now?' he asked.

'We've been to Kansas City to retrieve property belonging to Annette, Pa. So you watch what you say, or I'll bust you in the mouth, father or not. Clear?' Clay replied.

'You expect to stay here?' his father asked.

'I don't expect anything, Pa. We're on our way back to Texas, and I wanted to see my family. If you don't want us to stay, just say and we'll stay in town. We only plan to be around for a week, at the most.'

'Well, it's still Moon's farm, she'll want you to stay,' his father replied.

They all adjourned to the house for refreshments. There were two children, a boy about four and a girl of two, asleep in the parlour. The old lady had been minding them.

'Little Clay and Susan,' Judith told Annette.

'They are so beautiful,' Annette told the doting parents.

'Let's not stay if it's going to start a fight,' Annette said to Clay, when they were alone.

'Don't worry,' he told her. 'Pa wants us to stay. That's why he said that this is Moon's farm. This farm used to belong to Grandpa and Moon. My brothers are on what was Pa's farm.'

'Your mother and sister aren't very Indian-looking.'

'No, I got all the Indian blood, Moon says.'

For two days they just lazed around. Clay's brothers and their families came to visit. The women and children loved Clay; his brothers were very aloof, though. On the afternoon of the third day, Clay was playing hide and seek with the children, as Annette sat watching. The game was boisterous and usually ended up with everyone piled on top of Clay.

'I've got to rest a while,' he told them as he made his way to where Annette sat. To his surprise, she tried to hide the fact that she had been crying. 'What's the matter?' he asked.

'Oh nothing. It's just that, even after all that has happened, I'd still like to get married and have children, one day.'

Clay took her hands. 'You will, you will. One day you'll meet a nice young man, and all your dreams will come true.'

She looked at him despairingly. 'Who, Clay? Who'd want to marry me, after what happened? Who'd want to be the husband of a woman who was used by a gang of men? Who?'

'Annette,' Clay said softly, 'I would. I'd be honoured if you'd marry me.'

'Why, Clay?' Annette implored. 'Why would you do that?'

'Because I love you.'

She reached out and touched him on the cheek. 'Oh, Clay, I love you too, but I can't. I'm sorry.'

'Why not? Is it because I'm fourteen years

older than you? Do I look too Indian? What?'

'It's neither of those things, Clay. It's not you, it's me. It's because, at the present moment, I don't think that I could, you know, perform my wifely duty.'

Clay drew her to him and held her. 'Is that all? Look, I firmly believe that time is the great healer. I believe that one day you'll feel differently, and I want to be there when you do. Besides, it shouldn't be a duty for a woman. It should be something that two people do, because they love each other.' He looked into her eyes. 'I'll wait, Annette.'

'What if I can never do it?'

'Then it'll be a long, cold winter. For both of us. So?'

'Can I think about it?'

'No. The longer you think, the more excuses you'll come up with. So?'

She watched him through tear-filled eyes for what seemed like minutes.

'If I say yes, will you promise me something?'

'If you say yes, I'll promise you anything.'

'Will you promise me that if you need a woman, you'll find one. Just don't tell me about it, all right?'

Clay smiled, 'I'll promise you that. It'll never

happen, but I promise. So?'

Annette smiled and cried and laughed, all at the one time. 'All right, Clay. I'd be honoured to be your wife.'

Clay held her close, 'Will you make a promise too?'

'If I can.'

'I don't want you to be preoccupied with thoughts of whether things are going to happen. Will you promise me that?'

'I'll try, Clay. I'll promise you that.'

'Good. Now, may I kiss you?'

'Yes, you may.'

Hand in hand they ran to the house. Moon and Clay's mother and sister were ecstatic at the news.

They were wed in a simple ceremony, on the farm, one week later. Clay insisted on taking Annette to New York and Washington, for a honeymoon. 'You're a wealthy woman, Annette,' he told her. 'You can buy yourself all the latest fashions.'

She looked at him solemnly. 'Clay, I'm not a wealthy woman, we're a wealthy couple. I'll buy new dresses if you'll buy new suits.'

Clay picked her up and swung her around. 'Deal,' he replied.

Sixteen

Clay and Annette returned to El Paso in the middle of June. They stayed with Doctor and Mrs O'Day, who were absolutely thrilled to learn that they were married. Clay in no way alluded to the arrangement he had with Annette. He slept in a chair in their room. The doctor and his wife were overwhelmed by the gifts that Annette had bought them.

Before leaving for the ranch, Clay and Annette shopped for supplies. Clay was returning to the store, when he heard a woman's voice call, 'Clay.' He turned, to find himself face to face with Margot Devenish. 'I never thought I'd see you again. I'm very pleased to do so.'

'Thank you, Margot. How are you? How are your parents?'

123

'I'm well, thanks, so are my parents. Mother seems to have recovered best. I don't know, but I think that she may have always thought Bud would come to no good. As for Father, he's occupying himself, finding a husband for me.'

'You're going to let him?'

Margot shrugged. 'Why not? Mother married father when she hardly knew him. Her parents wanted someone to take over their land. It seems to have worked out for them, fairly well. Now father wants the same.'

'You're crazy if you let him do that to you,' Clay told her.

'Oh, well,' she replied. 'Look, now that we're not at odds, I'd still like to have that supper with you.'

'I can't, Margot. I'm sorry.'

'Why not?'

'Because I'm a married man.'

Margot seemed quite shocked. 'Well, well, I didn't know that. Your wife must be very understanding. You're off traipsing around the countryside, and she' s stuck God knows where.'

'My wife's here in Texas, Margot.'

Margot looked at him for a while, then she placed a hand on his arm.

'Look, Clay, I'd still like to see you. You're about

the only man I've ever felt attracted to. I'd be content being the other woman in your life. If father insists that I marry someone I don't love, at least I'd have you. God, I never thought I'd ever be having this conversation.'

Clay removed her hand. 'Shit, Margot, is that all you think of yourself? The other woman in my life? You're a beautiful, intelligent woman, but you need to put more value on yourself. You also don't understand what I'm telling you, or perhaps I'm not doing it very well. I'm in El Paso, because this is where my wife lives. I married Annette while we were visiting my family in Virginia.'

Margot paled noticeably. 'Well, congratulations. You married probably the richest woman in Texas.'

'I didn't marry her for money, Margot. It might be hard for you to understand, but I love Annette very much.'

Before he could continue, Annette burst out of the store.

'Clay, what are you doing?' she asked gaily. Her mood faded when she saw Margot. 'Oh, hello, Margot,' she said nervously.

'Hello, Annette. Clay told me your news. Congratulations. I hope you'll be very happy.'

'Thank you, Margot, we will be.'

Margot took her leave. Annette's enthusiasm had disappeared.

'Can you finish loading these supplies, please?' she asked.

Clay grabbed her by the arm. 'Hey, we were only talking.'

She looked at him for a while, then smiled self-consciously. 'I know, I'm sorry. It's just that, well, I feel that if I'm going to lose you to anyone, it would be to Margot.'

Clay held her to him. 'You won't lose me, Annette, believe me.'

'Deep down I know, Clay, but . . .'

'No buts, Annette. You've got me for life. Now, let's get this finished.'

They finished packing their supplies and were about to climb on to the wagon when a young man approached. He was wearing the sheriff's badge.

'Hello, Annette, Marshal,' he said. Annette introduced him to Clay. His name was Robert Wilkins.

'I'm the new sheriff,' he told them proudly. 'Marshal,' he asked rather shyly, 'I want to be the best sheriff I can possibly be. Do you have any advice for me?'

'If you like. You must be impartial. In a

dispute, listen to all sides of the story. It's all there in what people tell you. Doesn't matter if someone stumbles over their story, you listen. It's been my experience that in a dispute it's usually whoever yells the loudest who's in the wrong.'

'Thank you, Marshal.' He turned to Annette. 'Annette, when the marshal leaves, if you have any trouble at all, you come to me. Perhaps when you're settled, you might like to go to a church social one Saturday.'

Annette was embarrassed. 'Look, Robert, there's something you don't know. Clay isn't Marshal Blake, any more, he's just Mr Blake, and I'm Mrs Blake.'

Now the sheriff was embarrassed. 'I'm sorry, I didn't know. Congratulations.'

They both said, 'Thank you,' and watched the young man beat a hasty retreat.

'Should I expect more young men to come calling?' Clay asked.

Annette blushed. 'No. Look, Clay, before all this happened, I was quite a popular girl. But when I needed someone, you were the one who was there. You're the one I married, you're the one I love.'

Clay squeezed her hand, 'I know. Come on, let's go home.'

*

They drove out of town in silence. Both were aware that they were the subjects of considerable interest as they departed. It wouldn't be long before their marriage was the topic of conversation, all over El Paso.

'Tell me when we're on your land,' Clay said to Annette.

She squeezed his arm and rested her head on his shoulder. 'It's our land, Clay. Do you realize, that from now on, people will refer to Thistle as the Blake brand and Blake land?'

'Haven't thought about it. It seems a bit unfair. I'm not bringing a lot to this marriage.'

'Don't say that,' Annette rebuked him. 'I'd have nothing if it wasn't for you. Look, before we get home, there's something we need to talk about.'

Clay looked at her; he could see that she was embarrassed to say what was on her mind.

'You use your room. I'll sleep in your father's room.'

'How did you know it was that?'

'Just a guess.'

'I'm sorry, Clay. I know this must be very difficult for you.'

Clay put his arm around her and kissed her

softly. 'Don't worry about it. Remember your promise?'

'Yes. But what will we do, if someone finds out that we sleep in separate rooms?'

'Why would they? If we have visitors, they're not going to inspect the bedrooms. Besides, if someone should find out, I'll just say it's because you snore something terrible.'

Annette laughed.

Seventeen

A year passed. A year in which they both immersed themselves in the ranch. They hired three more hands and Annette delighted in teaching Clay what he needed to know to run a ranch.

Clay, in turn, was able to presuade Annette to resume a normal life. They were regulars at the church dances, even though the first time was very difficult for Annette. The whole hall just stared when they entered with Doctor and Mrs O'Day. Annette wore a light-blue dress that she had bought in New York. She looked stunning, Clay thought. As always, as she had been during her terrible ordeal, she was extremely dignified.

In the spring of '68, the Cattlemen's Association got up a herd to go to Kansas. Thistle sent two thousand head. This, plus very healthy returns from the saloon, made them very well off.

They were drafting out some bulls, when one of the hands drew their attention to a group of horsemen coming at a fast pace. Instantly, Annette was on the defensive and moved to stand with Clay.

The men were a posse out of El Paso, led by Sheriff Wilkins.

'I need to talk to you in private, Mr Blake,' the sheriff said.

'Sheriff, whatever you have to say, you can say in front of my wife,' Clay replied.

Sheriff Wilkins looked at Annette apprehensively, before speaking.

'Very well. Bud Devenish broke out of Yuma. He's on the run with three others. They're already in the county. They ransacked the Devenish home, looking for money. Colonel Devenish tried to take them and has been wounded. They took Margot hostage. I think they'll head for Mexico.'

Annette had her hands to her face and was crying when Clay took her in his arms.

'How long have you known this?' he asked.

'I didn't know. Not until a Circle D rider came for me and the doctor. I contacted the authorities in Yuma; they didn't think to inform us.

Apparently, there was a mass break out, plenty of dead, including Jack Hunt.'

'Well, that's something,' Clay said. 'Come up to the house.'

Clay had to lead Annette to the house, she was so shocked. 'He'll come here, Clay, I know he will,' she mumbled.

Pat Deacon, the wife of the first hand Annette had hired, came rushing in.

'Sit with her please, Pat,' Clay asked, and went to his room. He returned in ten minutes, wearing his gun and carrying his Henry rifle.

'What are you going to do?' the sheriff asked.

'I'm going after this bastard; he's not going to ruin Annette's life again. I'll do what I should have done the first time.'

Annette sprang from her chair, screaming, 'No! No!' as she threw herself into Clay's arms.

'Listen to me,' Clay said gently. 'We can't live like this. We can't be looking over our shoulders for the rest of our lives.'

'I don't want anything to happen to you,' Annette sobbed.

'Nothing will happen to me, my love. I'm Cherokee Blake, I see like an owl and hear like a fox, remember?'

'I remember.'

'Good. Now, what do you want to do? Stay here, or go to town?'

'I'll stay. They didn't drive me out before, they won't now.'

'Very well. Would you put some food together for me, please? I just want to talk to the sheriff and his men for a minute.'

The sheriff and Clay went outside. 'Can you leave some men here?' Clay asked.

'Yes. That's why I brought so many.'

'Thanks,' Clay said, then he turned to the men who waited expectantly. 'Thank you for coming, gentlemen. I appreciate your volunteering to stay here, to guard my wife and our home. But, there is something I have to say to you. Annette is very easily frightened by strange men. If anyone does anything to frighten her, I'll kill him. I know this is a terrible thing to say to men who came with the best of intentions, but Annette's welfare is more important than anyone's hurt feelings. Is that clear?' No one answered.

The sheriff took Clay aside. 'I should be the one to go after Bud,' he said.

'Sheriff, you have a lot to do. If Bud goes out of the county, you don't have any more authority than I do.'

'I suppose. This is what I've done, tell me what

you think. I've sent riders to all the outlying ranches and settlements, urging them to try to gather in the one place, or at the least, to stay home and be ready. Should I do anything else?'

'That's about all you can do. Best you go back to town. Keep your horse ready to run. If you get a report on these men, try to imagine where they're headed for, and see if you can cut them off. Above all, don't let anyone bully you into deploying your men in the one place, or too thinly all over the place. There' s virtually nothing you can do, until these men are sighted. Just keep a level head, you'll do fine.'

Clay went to the barn to saddle his horse. He was joined by a tall, young cowhand, who was nervously fingering his hat.

'Mr Blake, I want to come with you,' he said.

'You ever killed anyone, son?' Clay asked.

'No, sir.'

'Then you're not much use to me. I'm going with the intention of killing Bud and his friends, I can manage that alone.'

'Mr Blake, you don't understand, I'd happily die for Margot.'

Clay looked at the forlorn young man.'What's your name?' he asked.

'Joe Foster, sir.'

'And you're in love with Margot.'

'Yes, sir.'

'She know this?'

'No, sir. I'm only a cowhand. She's engaged to Edward Ross. His family owns land from here to New Mexico, near enough.'

'Where's this Edward Ross, now?'

'He's at the ranch, looking after the colonel.'

'Um-m. Sounds like Mr Ross should be engaged to the colonel. I'll tell you something, young Joseph. If there's one thing in this world that Margot needs more than being rescued from her crazy brother, it's to know that someone loves her just for herself. Very well, you can come, but you do as you're told. Clear?'

'Yes, sir.'

'For God's sake, don't call me Mr Blake, or sir. It's Clay, got that? Clay.'

'Yes, sir.'

'Shit. Come to the house.'

In the house, Clay decided on a plan of action. He didn't really know where the Circle D ranch house was, compared to the Thistle ranch house. He was informed that it was about the same distance north-east of El Paso, as Thistle was north-west. Joe estimated that it was probably twenty miles from one house to the other. In between, there were hills and some gulch country.

'I'd expect them to head into the hills,' Clay told Joe and the sheriff.

'Why do you think that?' Joe asked.

'Because Bud knows this country like the back of his hand. They know that every gun in El Paso will be waiting for them to run for the border. So they'll hole up for a while.'

'We could throw all the men on to their trail,' the sheriff suggested.

'They'll spot a posse a mile off. Bud might be a bit crazy, but don't make the mistake of thinking he's stupid. He won't run for Mexico without coming here. He blames me and Annette for sending him to jail, and he wants to kill us. Revenge is on his mind, just as much as escaping.'

'Then why did he take Margot? They always got on well, apparently,' Joe asked.

'Insurance, probably. Trouble is, how long before his companions decide that they want Margot more than they need Bud.'

While they were talking, Annette had pulled herself together enough to help Pat serve coffee and bread and jam to the four men who were staying. Clay knew that it was a tremendous effort for her to socialize with these people, and he was very proud of her for doing so.

Now it was time to go. Annette walked with Clay to his horse.

'How long will you be gone?' she queried.

'Long as it takes. Two, three days,' he replied.

Annette took his hand in hers. 'Clay . . .' she started to say.

'Now's not the time, baby,' he told her gently. 'I have to do this, you know that, don't you?'

'Yes, I know.'

'Well, when I get back, if you need to talk, we'll talk.'

'All right.'

'Good.' He took her in his arms. 'You remember that I love you. There's nothing that we can't work out, if necessary. And no one's going to ruin our lives, not Bud, no one.'

'I know, Clay. I love you too. You've no idea how much I rely on you and appreciate what you've done for me.'

Clay kissed her. 'Thank you, Annette. Now, you stay calm, and I'll be back before you know it.'

Clay mounted up and he and Joe rode off.

The two men rode due east, skirting the hills.

'How far do you think we've come?' Clay asked Joe.

'About fifteen miles.'

'Yes, that's my reckoning. We'll head into the hills now, and see if we can cut their trail.'

They found nothing that evening, so they bedded down in a cave, where they could build a fire to brew their coffee.

At sun-up they were on their way again. About noon they came across a trail of what Clay estimated to be five or six horses, heading slightly north of west.

'If it's them, where are they headed?' Joe asked.

'I reckon they're heading west until Bud thinks that they're due north of Thistle. Then they'll turn south, kill me and Annette, and make a run for the border. Come on.'

Shortly before sundown they came upon fresh horse droppings. Clay broke some up in his hands.

'Just a few hours old,' he told Joe. 'Leave the horses.'

They walked for about an hour before finding five people camped under a rock overhang.

'That them?' Joe asked.

'Think so,' Clay replied. 'Yes, there's Margot, cooking something.'

'What do we do?' Joe asked.

'Light's not good enough now, we'll hit them in the morning.'

Joe and Clay were in position before dawn. Bud and his companions weren't in any hurry. The sun was well up before anyone stirred. Margot put pans on the fire, water on to boil, then headed for the stream. '*Señorita*, do you need a hand?' they heard someone say.

'You leave her alone,' they heard Bud reply.

Clay turned to Joe. 'You go and grab Margot. Keep her quiet and get her away quickly,' he said, as he unsheathed his Henry rifle.

'You sure you don't need a hand?' Joe asked.

'No, I'll be fine. Go on.'

Joe hurried away, keeping low. He found Margot by the stream, dipping a towel into the water. He got as close as he could, then rushed out, clamped a hand over her mouth, and dragged her into the bushes. Margot struggled like a demon.

'It's Joe Foster, Miss Margot,' Joe whispered in her ear. 'You're safe now. Please don't scream when I take my hand away.'

Joe removed his hand. Margot looked at him for a moment, then threw her arms around his neck.

'Thank you, Joe. I was petrified.' she said into his neck.

Joe held her tight. 'You're safe now, miss.'

'Who else is with you?' Margot asked.

'Clay Blake, miss.'

Margot looked at Joe. 'Clay? Where's he?'

'He's at the camp, miss.'

Margot buried her head in Joe's neck again. 'Oh, my God,' she whispered.

Clay watched the four men. They all made trips into the bushes, so he waited until they were all gathered at the fire. There was Bud, another white man and two more, who looked like Mexicans or part-Indians. Two sat on their bedrolls, Bud and one of the darker men stood. Clay moved to where he could see the men if they ran for the rock overhang, then he opened fire. He took the two standing men first. One shot each through the chest, in the region of their hearts. One reclining man was partly on his feet when a bullet similarly placed killed him.

The remaining man had the presence of mind to squirm into the bushes, only inches in front of a bullet. Clay moved to where he could see the trail the man made, estimated how far he could have crawled, and sent two more bullets after him. There was a scream, then an accented voice said, 'I give up, *Señor*.'

'Come out, hands raised,' Clay called. The man stood, one hand holding a six-gun. Clay shot him dead. Then there was silence. Clay walked to where the men lay. Bud was still alive and bleeding severely from a chest wound. He tried to speak but couldn't. Clay hunkered down beside him.

'Burn in hell, you bastard,' he said. Bud's eyes slowly glazed over and he was gone.

When the shooting stopped, Joe took Margot's hand and headed back to the camp. They found Clay inspecting the bodies.

'Oh, God,' Margot said and tried to go to her brother.

Clay blocked her way. 'He's dead, Margot,' he said matter of factly.

'Did you have to kill him? Couldn't you have captured him?'

'Then what?' Clay asked sharply. 'Send him back to Yuma, so he could hang? He's dead now, Margot, it's finished. We'll load them up and take them back to town. Perhaps your parents might like to bury their son in your family plot.'

Margot looked contrite and wiped the tears from her eyes.

'I'm sorry, Clay, I shouldn't be angry with you. Deep down I knew it would come to this. I prayed you'd come, I was scared stiff of those men. At least Bud wouldn't let them touch me.'

'Then remember that, Margot. Remember that when it counted, he was still a good brother. But remember this too, if you were scared, try to imagine how Annette felt. Understand why she wanted revenge. Understand this too. I came to kill Bud. I wasn't going to let him spoil our lives, any more than he has.'

'I know, Clay, but I'll always think that you came for me.'

'Look, Margot, don't see things that aren't there. Besides, Joe tells me you're engaged to Edward Ross.'

'Yes.'

'You must be out of your damned mind,' Clay told her forcefully. 'You have a lot to offer a man. You have your whole life in front of you and you're letting this happen. If your fiancé was any sort of a man, he'd be here rescuing you. Instead, he's home and Joe's here.'

Margot looked at the blushing Joe. 'Why are you here, Joe?' she asked.

'Someone had to come, Miss Margot,' he replied softly.

142

'Shit!' Clay exclaimed. 'You two are the most hopeless pair of bastards I've ever met. 'He's here because he loves you, Margot. He'd gladly die for you. Isn't that what you said, Joe?'

'Yes, sir,' Joe mumbled.

'So you see, Margot,' Clay continued. 'Someone can love you without trying to impress your father. If you'd stop wallowing in self-pity, perhaps you'd see it yourself. Now, do you think between you, you could help saddle these horses? I want to get home to my wife.'

Before setting out, Clay and Joe ate the beans and bacon that Margot had been preparing. She sat forlornly, clutching a cup of coffee and occassionally wiping away a tear.

Clay and Joe loaded the bodies on to the horses. Clay removed the bridle and saddle from one horse, and let it go. 'You ride double with Joe,' he told Margot and gave Joe a wink as he legged her up.

People stood silently in the street and watched the macabre procession pass by. Clay reined in at the sheriff's office. Sheriff Wilkins and several of his deputies spilled out on to the sidewalk.

'Shit,' the sheriff said to no one. Then to his men he said, 'Take them to the undertaker's.'

Clay dismounted and Joe helped Margot down.

'You all right, miss?' the sheriff asked.

'Yes, thank you,' Margot replied.

Before anyone said anything else, someone called, 'Blake!'

They all turned to see former deputy Roy Wallace standing in the middle of the street.

'Yes?' Clay answered.

'You think you're a hard man when you're armed with a shotgun or rifle. How tough are you with just a handgun?'

'Don't do this, Roy,' the sheriff said.

'Stay out of this, Sheriff. This is between the 'breed and me,' Roy answered vehemently.

Clay moved into the street. 'Well, Roy,' he said, 'I think I'm passable. I suppose you're the fastest gun in Texas, right?'

'You're about to find out,' Roy replied and went for his gun.

He had barely started to draw, when he found himself looking down the barrel of Clay's .45.

'Surpri-ise, Roy,' Clay said, as he stood with his gun cocked and rock-steady. Roy stood, hypnotized by the gun pointing at him. 'Keep going,' Clay goaded.

'No. You'll kill me.'

Clay smiled. 'Well, Roy, I'll tell you what, take

144

your gun out, real slowly.' Roy did so. 'Now cock it and hold it down at your side.' When Roy had done this, Clay dropped the hammer of his own gun, spun it on his finger and reholstered it. 'All right, Roy, my friend, I'll give you a start. When you're ready, you try it. You might be fast enough, you might get me. But understand this. I will kill you, there's absolutely no doubt about that. So welcome to the last half-minute of your life. Go on, do it, show everyone how tough you are.'

Roy looked panic-stricken.

'No, no,' he mumbled and threw his gun on the ground.

Clay just stood. 'You're pathetic, Roy, do you know that? Do you think I lasted as long as I did as a marshal, without being good with a gun? The only reason I carried a shotgun, was I had no intention of being shot dead by some loud-mouthed bastard like you. Now, what do I do about you? I'm not going to be worrying about you for the rest of my life.'

'I'm leaving, I'm leaving,' Roy pleaded.

'See that you do. If I ever see you again, I'll kill you. Clear?'

'Yes,' Roy replied and hurried away.

'You forgot your gun,' Clay yelled after him. He kept on going.

'Shit,' Sheriff Wilkins said.

Clay smiled at the young sheriff. 'There's the best lesson I can teach you, Sheriff. Don't get drawn into gunfights. Never underestimate anyone. Get a shotgun and carry it all the time. The secret to being a good lawman is being a live lawman. Do you think you're fast with a gun?'

'Good enough.'

'As fast as me? Be honest, now.'

The sheriff smiled. 'Not as fast as you, but faster than he was.'

'Well then, here's something else I can teach you. There's only the blink of an eye between someone who's just good and someone who is really fast. The best shot will always come out on top, always. How wide do you think Main Street is?'

'Oh, forty yards?'

'Near enough. Do you know that, at that distance, eight out of ten men won't hit you? Half of them won't be able to see you.'

'No, I didn't know that.'

'Well it's true. Practise on a target forty yards away. If you have to go against someone in a gunfight, pull them up at that distance, then you'll have the edge. But avoid that. Always have your shotgun in reach. Do what I did, get a gunsmith to make something to fit over the hammers. If you're in a bad situation, tie the triggers back, then hold the hammers back with your thumb. Even the silliest bastard in the world isn't going to shoot you when he knows you'll blow him apart even if you're dead.'

'Yes, sir, thank you,' the sheriff answered. 'Incidentally, there's a ten thousand dollar reward for the capture of those men. Apparently, they murdered five cowhands, to get horses and supplies.'

'Damn them to hell,' Clay replied. 'I don't want the money. Give four thousand to Joe, then divide the rest up amongst your deputies.'

'If you wish. Times are tough, the men will appreciate that.'

Clay moved to where Margot and Joe stood. 'Well, I'll get on home. Will you be all right?'

'Clay, would you do me a tremendous favour?' Margot asked rather sheepishly.

'What?'

'Would you come home with me? I'm going to have it out with father, once and for all. I need all the support I can get.'

'I suppose. I won't be able to go to your place, and then get home by tonight. We'd best stay in town and go on in the morning.'

'Thank you.'

Clay told them that he would stay at the O'Days. He told Joe to arrange for a rider to go to the Circle D, and tell Mr and Mrs Devenish that Margot was safe. He also told Joe to book himself and Margot into the hotel, then take her out to supper.

'I don't have any money,' Joe said bashfully.

Clay feinted a punch at him and gave him twenty dollars.

Eighteen

They were ready to move out early.

'Have a nice evening?' Clay asked Margot, as they were saddling up.

'Yes, I did. Are you satisfied? Yes!' she answered defiantly. It was obvious that Margot was happy to ride double with Joe. Clay tried not to smile as he legged her up.

It was just before noon when they arrived at the Circle D. Mr and Mrs Devenish had hurried from the house when one of the hands told them that riders were coming in. They were accompanied by a plump man about five feet ten inches tall. Edward Ross, Clay surmised.

Margot was welcomed very emotionally by her parents. They were obviously upset by what had happened and by the death of their son.

Edward Ross took Margot by the arm.

'Come to the house, my dear,' he said.

Margot shook herself loose. 'Let me go,' she said forcefully. To her father, she said, 'Father, I won't marry this man.'

'It's the best thing for you, Margot,' her father replied. 'We won't discuss this in front of strangers.'

'Yes we will, Father. Clay and Joe rescued me. Where was Edward? Here protecting his inheritance. Father, I'm twenty-five years old. I know as much about running this ranch as anyone. If you want to leave the ranch to this, this clod, do so. But I warn you here and now, I'll contest it in every court in the land. And you certainly aren't going to give me to him. So choose now, him or me.'

'You're distraught, Margot. We'll discuss this later,' Edward Ross said. Again he took her by the arm.

'Don't touch me, you cringing slug. Do you know what the girls call you at dances? Mr Creepy. When you touch me, I shudder.' She turned to her father. 'Well, Father?'

'Whatever you wish, Margot,' her father softly replied.

'You can't do this,' Edward Ross said to James Devenish.

Fire came back into the old man's eyes. 'Yes I can. If this is what Margot wants, it's what she will have. Now, get out.'

Edward Ross stormed away. Margot hugged her father.

'Thank you, Poppa,' she said. She turned to Clay, 'Well?' she asked.

'That was good, real good.' He kissed her on the cheek. 'You go along, now.'

'I'm in your debt for ever, Clay,' she said. She turned to Joe. 'Joseph, would you join us for supper this evening, please?'

Joe was dumbfounded. 'Yes, Margot, I'd be honoured.'

Margot headed to the house, with her mother.

'Thank you, Mr Blake,' Clay heard James Devenish say.

'I didn't go for Margot. I went to kill Bud.'

'I know. That was inevitable, I suppose. But you brought Margot back.'

'She's a fine young woman, Devenish. Give her a chance. Annette can run her ranch extremely well. No reason Margot can't do the same.'

'Well I'll certainly give her the chance. How's Annette?'

'She's fine, thank you.'

'Then I'm pleased.'

'She doesn't blame you. You didn't do anything to her.'

'I know. Both my wife and I feel that we'd like to talk to her. But what do you say in a case like this? It was our son. How did it happen? What did we do wrong?'

'I don't know. I've heard hundreds of parents ask the same question, but I don't have the answer. Bud's dead now. Mourn your son and get on with your life. That's all I can tell you.'

'Thank you,' the older man said emotionally.

'Why don't you and your family visit some time?' Clay asked. 'It might be awkward at first. But I think it would do you all the world of good, to talk to one another.'

'Very well, we will.'

'Good. Well, I'll see you, Colonel,' Clay said as he reined away.

James Devenish smiled. 'Yes, see you, Clay.'

Nineteen

Clay arrived home about dusk. He was perturbed by the fact that he wasn't challenged when he was in view of the house. He put his horse in the barn and gave him an extra dipper of oats.

As he neared the porch, he heard laughter from inside the house. He entered, to find the deputies and all the hands being served supper by Annette and Pat Deacon.

'Shouldn't someone be on guard?' he asked.

Annette placed a saucepan back on the stove and hurried to him.

'The sheriff sent a rider to tell us what happened. Are you all right?' she asked nervously.

'Yea, I'm fine. I'll just wash up and put some bath water on.'

Clay went to the bathroom and washed. When

he turned to light the boiler, Annette was standing in the doorway.

'That rider who came this morning. He said that you went home with Margot.'

'That's right.'

'Why, Clay? Don't you think I was worried about you? And you're off with Margot.'

Clay lit the boiler and put a bit of wood in it before he turned his attention to Annette.

'Is our first argument going to be about Margot Devenish?' he asked.

'Yes, Clay, I think it is.'

'Well then, I can assure you that there's no reason to argue. Besides, it looks as though you're enjoying yourself.'

Annette was rather taken aback by this.

'That's not fair. It's very hard for me to socialize with these men. I've tried my best, I hoped you'd be proud of me.'

Clay folded her in his arms.

'I am, I am,' he said. 'I'm sorry, that wasn't the right thing to say. I rode home with Margot and Joe because Margot needed moral support to confront her father. He was insisting that she marry someone named Edward Ross. Do you know him?'

'Mr Creepy? He's awful. How could she let that happen?'

'That's what I asked. Anyway, she told her old man that she wouldn't marry him. The colonel sent him packing. That Joe Foster is mad about her. He's a nice fellow. Perhaps that'll work out.'

'Yes, Joe is nice.'

Clay let her go. 'Well, that's it. She was in trouble, so I helped her out. For no other reason than she's a nice young woman who needed help. Believe it or not, Margot is quite insecure and very lonely. She doesn't seem to have any friends.'

'Except you,' Annette said defiantly.

'Yes, except me. Is that what you want me to say?'

In the half-light, Clay could see that Annette's eyes were shiny, she was close to tears. Again he took her in his arms.

'I'm sorry, Annette. Look, I went twenty miles out of my way to help Margot. Believe me I when I say that I wanted to get home to you. But it seemed like the thing to do. Do, you remember where I said I was when I was asked to look into your case? After several marshals here in Texas refused to do anything about it, I might add.'

'No.'

'I was in Chicago. I went from there to Kansas City, then on to here. That must be what, fifteen hundred miles? I came all that way for a total stranger; twenty miles for a friend doesn't seem like much of an effort.'

'I didn't know that.'

'Well, now you do. Look, I'm hungry and tired. I'd like to have some supper, then go to bed. Come on.' He took her hand and they returned to the kitchen.

The men in the kitchen were preparing to leave. They thanked Annette for her hospitality, and thanked Clay for donating the reward money to them. Then they left.

The Deacons and the hands departed and Clay sat alone eating a dish of stew, as Annette cleaned up.

'I'll have a bath and go to bed, if you don't mind,' Clay said.

'Do as you like,' Annette replied, a trifle abruptly.

Twenty

Clay stood at his dressing table with a towel wrapped around him. He brushed his hair and tied it back the way he preferred to wear it. 'Am I becoming more Indian?' he asked his reflection. Something touched him softly on the back. He half-turned to find Annette standing there.

'Hell, Annette, you scared the life out of me.'

She laughed throatily. 'What happened to hear like a fox and see like an owl?'

Clay had to smile in spite of himself.

'Even animals sleep. Now, what do you want? You shouldn't be in here.'

'It's my house, Clay. Why shouldn't I come in here?'

'Yes, it's your house. So, what do you want?'

'I want to talk.' Clay went to turn around. 'No,

157

don't turn around, please. It'll be easier for me to talk to your back.'

'Very well. Let me guess, you don't think things are working out, so you'd like me to move on. Am I right?'

There was silence for a while. When Annette answered, it was in a strained whisper.

'Good God, Clay, no. Why on earth do you think that?'

'I dreamt it; several times, in fact. Now, with all this Margot business, I thought you'd want me gone.'

'Clay, you're my husband and I love you. I apologize for what I said about you and Margot. Especially considering the promise I had you make, when you proposed to me. It's just that, well, Margot and I used to be very good friends. I'd hate to lose my husband to her.'

'Well, you won't, Annette. I've told you that a hundred times. You should try to be friends with her again. As a matter of fact, I suggested to the colonel that they visit some time. It would do them the world of good if you told them they're not to blame.'

'I don't blame them. You know that.'

'That's what I told the colonel. But I think he needs to hear it from you. It won't do you any harm to talk to them.'

'All right.'

'Good. Now, I want to go to bed. Under the circumstances, it's not a good idea for you to come in here, when I'm not dressed.' Clay felt her hand move across his back again. 'Damn it, Annette, don't do that!' he yelled. 'It's hard enough living the way we do, without you playing silly games.'

'Don't be angry, please, Clay. There's something I want to tell you, and I'm very nervous.'

Clay felt for her. 'I'm sorry, baby. There's no need to be nervous, just tell me.'

She paused before she finally blurted it out.

'Clay, I want us to be man and wife in every sense of the words. I've been trying to tell you for a month or more. I've stood outside your door, half a dozen times, recently, but I just haven't been able to take that final step, until now. I'm sorry. I know that things have been terribly hard for you and I apologize. You were right about one thing, time heals all things. Now, I would like us to have a family, then my life would be perfect.'

Clay turned to her. In the lamplight she looked vulnerable and defenceless. He took her in his arms.

'You don't need to apologize for anything, Annette. We knew that it would take time. But you've got to be one hundred per cent sure. I'd hate it, if I frightened you.'

'You won't, my love. You've never frightened me. So, would you mind turning the lamp down, while I get into bed?'

When Clay awoke, sunlight was filtering through the window. He was alone. He dressed and went to the kitchen. Annette was at the stove, cooking breakfast and humming softly. She turned to the table and saw Clay standing in the doorway. She curtsied slightly.

'Good morning, husband,' she said.

'Good morning, wife,' Clay replied. 'How are you today?'

'I feel marvellous, thank you. I feel, I don't know, liberated, something like that.'

'That's good.'

'Yes. Look, I gave all the hands a month's pay and a week off. I thought it would be nice if we could just spend some time together. Is that all right?'

Clay took her in his arms. 'That sounds marvellous,' he said.